From the Reviews of
The Girl Green as Elderflower

About the Author

Randolph Stow was born in 1935 at Geraldton, Western Australia, and educated at Guildford Grammar School and the University of Western Australia. After working on a mission station for Australian Aborigines, he studied anthropological linguistics at the University of Sydney and Indonesian languages at Yale University. He then went as a Cadet Patrol Officer to Papua New Guinea, where he was assistant to the Government Anthropologist. Since 1960 he has lived mainly in England, though he has travelled widely in Europe, North America, and Asia.

In 1979 he won the Patrick White Award, given annually to the writer whose body of work is considered to have made a distinguished contribution to Australian literature. Mr. Stow's other novels include *Visitants* (Taplinger, 1981), *To the Islands* (Taplinger, rev. edn., 1982), and *Tourmaline* (Taplinger, 1983; first American publication of this 1963 novel). In 1984 Taplinger published *The Suburbs of Hell* and reissued Mr. Stow's 1965 work, *The Merry-Go-Round in the Sea*.

The Girl Green as
Elderflower

Also by Randolph Stow

Novels

A HAUNTED LAND
THE BYSTANDER
TO THE ISLANDS
TOURMALINE
THE MERRY-GO-ROUND IN THE SEA
THE SUBURBS OF HELL
VISITANTS

Poetry

ACT ONE
OUTRIDER
A COUNTERFEIT SILENCE

For Children

MIDNITE

RANDOLPH STOW

The Girl Green as Elderflower

TAPLINGER PUBLISHING COMPANY
NEW YORK

First paperback edition published in 1984 by
TAPLINGER PUBLISHING CO., INC.
New York, New York

Copyright © 1980 by Julian Randolph Stow
Reprinted by arrangement with The Viking Press,
40 West 23rd Street, New York, New York 10010

LIBRARY OF CONGRESS CATALOGING IN PUBLICATION DATA

Stow, Randolph, 1935–
    The girl green as elderflower.

    I. Title.
PR9619.S84G5   1984   823   84-8905
ISBN 0-8008-3269-8 (pbk.)

Printed in the United States of America

To C. in Suffolk

Even such midnight years
must ebb; bequeathing this:
a dim low English room,
one window on the fields.

Cloddish ancestral ghosts
plod in a drowning mist.
Black coral elms play host
to hosts of shrill black fish.

*My mare turns back her ears
and hears the land she leaves
as grievous music.*

'OUTRIDER' (1960)

The Girl Green as Elderflower

JANUARY

Quite how to go about doing it Clare could still not see, but the impression was strong with him that the doing would be important, might even be the rebeginning of his health. That idea of health was all but novel to him, he had sunk so deep, and it presented itself with an urgent attractiveness in the new year's astonishing first white light.

Through a window to his right the old unpruned apple tree which had gathered wreaths of snow in its mossy twigs was being shocked free of them by the spurts of little dun birds. The two rising fields behind, one pasture and one plough, were today unbroken by any tussock or ridge of conker-coloured earth, and lay so uniformly white and unshadowed that it seemed that they must be uniformly level. In the distance, across the river, a line of bare poplars on a ridge was caught in an odd spotlight of sun, and stood out against the heavy sky with an unEnglish sharpness, shining through air from which all moisture had frozen and fallen.

The other window was directly before him as he lay in bed, and indeed he had aligned the bed, in the summer, so that by moonlight he could look down the clearing of the abandoned fishponds, with their nettle-choked sluices, to the *Sylphides*-like wood which closed the view. When he had come to the cottage it had seemed that his stay would not be long, and for furniture in that room he had brought only a bed, a table, a lamp and a painting which Alicia had done. It hung on the pale yellow wall like a third window, giving a view of what would have been seen from such a window in August, when chickens went scratching about the barley-stubble. In the snow-light so much gold and green was almost garish. His eye strayed from that down the nettle-borne humps of snow to the black and white wood, in which an occasional holm oak, holly or clump of tree-ivy was only slightly green in its darkness.

A morning-after thirst was on him, and he slid out a hand for water. The flexible plastic beaker was rigid. What was in it was ice. He found himself laughing at this exotic turn, and sitting up in bed crushed the beaker between his hands until he had freed some water from its centre.

His pyjama jacket was damp. It had been another fever-night. In the freezing room the jacket seemed likely to turn to ice on his back, and he tore it off and buried himself again in the warmed sheets.

On the low table beside him a fat book was propped against a squatter one, a dictionary. His eye drifted over words he had been reading before going to sleep, and began pleasantly to unfocus. Rolling over, he tried deliberately to bring back the dream which must have had to do, somehow, with that page: the fever-dream. In his room full of icy light, its open windows (for he had grown unused to white men's houses) commanding a leafless landscape, he tried to recreate the face which had appeared to him: a face made of summer leaves, not sinister but pitilessly amused. When he had woken, it had been with the Green Man's voice in his ears, actually within the bones of the ear, supernaturally loud. Though he could not recapture the voice, he felt again his vague affright, for it was internal as sound never was. And it had spoken to him, he thought he now remembered, in that language in which he so often dreamed, and would not hear spoken again. But the sense of the speech eluded him. Only the tone reverberated, amused beyond the reach of pity.

The dawn of a new year. He caught himself groaning: 'Avaka bavagi baesa?' and mentally, with embarrassment,

4

translated. It half-woke him, that slip. It was a question, in English, of plans for the future, of picking up pieces which had been broken desperately small.

When he had almost descended into the world where the voice belonged a bell rang in the bowels of the earth. Downstairs the telephone was clamouring through closed doors, and the unaccustomed urgency of the noise shocked him out of his bed and had him halfway down the breakneck stairs before the cold fastened about his bare torso. At the foot of the stairs he grabbed a donkey-jacket, and was struggling into it as he burst into the room which served him as a study. He seized the clangorous telephone.

It said nothing. After a moment, still shivering and writhing in the jacket, he ventured: 'Clare.'

A child's voice said: 'Is that you?'

'Is that who?' Clare asked. 'This is Sandringham 123, Duke of Edinburgh speaking. She can't come to the phone, I'm afraid, she's making a snowman at the moment.'

Suddenly he saw a snowman with a face of frost-ferns, ruthlessly entertained.

'I know it's you, Crispin,' the child said.

'I knew it was you, Mikey,' said Clare. 'Does your mother want to speak to me?'

There was a pause, then Mikey said: 'Well, she says yes. But it's Fred really. He's the one who wants to talk to you.'

'And who is Fred?' Clare inquired.

'The one on the ouija board,' Mikey said. 'You know: Fred.'

'Oh, him,' Clare said. 'People as boring as Fred shouldn't be allowed on the ouija board. This is a funny time of day for that, anyway.'

'It was last night really,' Mikey explained, 'but we did it again this morning, and he said the same. We asked him if there was someone he wanted to talk to, and he wrote C–R–I–S, both times. We rang you last night to ask you to come and talk to him, but you were out getting sloshed.'

'Fred knew that?' Clare marvelled.

5

'No, Marco said. He saw you in the White Hart. He's sick today.'

There was some faint agitation on the line, then a girl's voice, older than the boy's, said: 'Crispin?'

'Yes, Lucy.'

'He wanted to be the one to ring you up, but he really doesn't understand. Stop it, Mikey. It's different, because of Amabel.'

'That fairy-child,' Clare said. 'I can believe it's different. I suppose she wouldn't be faking it?'

From the silence at the other end he guessed that Amabel was in the room, and answered himself: 'No, she's too young.'

'It's not that silly old soldier any more,' Lucy said. 'I don't know who it is, but it writes ever so fast for Amabel. Even with Marco she's got some sentences, and Marco's thick that way.'

'And your mother?' Clare asked.

'She won't touch it, not with Amabel. I think she's changing her mind about it.'

'Aha,' he said. A saying of Alicia Clare's was: Things probably *are* what they seem. Finding her daughter's friends using a ouija board as a toy, she was pleased to think that they had got its measure. Now she was being tested by uncanny, elfin Amabel.

'Do come,' Lucy said. 'Amabel's father is fetching her after supper. Mummy says come to tea.'

Well, yes,' said Clare. 'Thank her. Or the ouija board. Is something wrong with Mikey?'

Mikey's sister puffed a sigh and muttered daringly: '*Bloody* child.'

'I see,' Clare said. 'Or no doubt shall.' Oddly, the exercise of freezing to death was starting rivulets of ice water from his armpits. 'Lucy, I'll perish if I don't light a fire in here. So goodbye to you for now.'

On the hearth stood a brimming bucket of coals; there were logs and kindling. In a minute flamelight was dancing over him. He crouched, waiflike, among his sticks of secondhand furniture, his spirit disciplined by the formalities of a wallpaper chosen, in another age, by a stockman's wife as suitable for Sundays. In that room both windows were filled with the spun-glass intricacies of a lilac hedge, as pure and chilling, to his eye, as a map of veins and arteries in a textbook. But even that deathly complexity seemed less inimical to man when the coal released its gases and the light began to change colour.

He sat on the mat with his knees drawn up inside the jacket. So Mikey was throwing his pygmy weight around, and one could understand that, poor kid. But another worry for Alicia, a worry with no sure term to it.

But he, for the moment, could only think of the happiness of his body, his fibres unclenching in the warmth. Fire, the ancestral god. And as the kindling spat at him and he stirred, he seemed to glimpse once more the god's face, the smile unchanging, whether sketched by leaves or by flame.

At the top of the hill he turned, breathing deep and white, and looked back, down the pits of blue shadow which were his footprints, to the smoking cottage at the heart of the curved waste of white and grey. All the light in the landscape was drawn to its red bricks. Modest as it was, it imposed by its colour, seeming to tower. Except for the hedgerows, it was the only sign of man.

A mincing cock-pheasant examined the holes his Wellingtons had made, and suddenly, as if acting on information, a swarm of sparrows and blackbirds came to do the same. The light changed. In the sky which had been lowering there were patches of a tender summery blue.

The Hole Farm, generations of Clares had called that narrow valley. Their farmhouse lay, hidden by trees, near the source of the stream which had formed it. To their descendant, transient tenant of the tied cottage, the honest old yokel name had always seemed picturesque as sneezewort or fleabane. But the Clares had long ago left the yokel life, and their successors in the farmhouse by the stream gave an address more dignified than The Hole.

Two ponies which had been standing under an oak came

with careful steps, as if the snow hid traps, to see what was in his pockets. Their rough hides, chestnut and bay, glowed in that light, organic as a blush. He had nothing to share with them but his warmth, which they seemed to savour. One of them belonged to Lucy.

He closed the gate on the farm and went up a noiseless white lane towards the village, emerging near the church. On the footpath between the headstones there was not a mark. Once again he noted the spikiness of the churchyard greenery, in which yew, holly and mahonia predominated, all in this weather formidable as ironmongery.

By the further gate he passed Crispin Clare of The Hole Farm. Some memory of that stone, accidentally prominent, must have led Major Clare to give his son the same name. The siting of a footpath had brought the old farmer and malster fame, and to his great-great-great-grandson Swainsteadian visitors at Martlets would say: 'Not *Crispin* Clare?' 'Ah, him that live up the boonyard,' young Mark Clare would mumble, in the dialect he affected. 'That old booy that creep out at midnight and suck Mikey's blood.' At that Mikey would shriek: 'Shut up, shut up, shut up, Marco,' delighted. He knew about vampires from television, and toyed with his mysterious cousin, suddenly materialized out of the world at large, like Cleopatra exploring the possibilities of the asp.

There was a twinkling weatherfastness about Swainstead in the snow. Since the late Middle Ages, when it had prospered on the trade in woollens, it had been a substantial village, almost a town, and its substantial houses suggested no want of anything comfortable, ever. After the Clares had left the soil for the law and other professions, a solicitor among them who had thrived announced the fact by buying the house he most admired in his native place. Martlets was not grand, but it had about it the weight and confidence of money, with another quality which money could buy, a high-handed stance towards time. Cloth had built it in the fifteenth century, as cloth had built so many great churches in the countryside around, and although it had sprouted a wing since then, the old clothier

8

might still have recognized his rooms. To Clare at the age of nine it had seemed a rather dull museum, reprehensibly cold. But to his father, son of a poor colonial clergyman and lately reappeared from having a good war, it was clear that young Crissie ought to wander a little in his own boyhood haunts, and in that determination he was strengthened by the chance of the boy's being on the mother's side, too, a son of the house. For Mrs Clare, though as unmetropolitan as a solar topee, had been a Melford; and the Melford arms, bought in the seventeenth century with the profits from their excellent cloth, gave Martlets its name. So, on a chill grey post-war day, the boy was presented to his great-uncle, a heron of a man with family solicitor written all over him, and to the great-uncle's wife, in tweed skirt and twin-set from which pearls were not missing, and to the great-uncle's son, partner and neighbour Charles, whose young wife was called Alicia and whose three-year-old firstborn was Marco. And from then till his catastrophe he had not seen or thought of Swainstead, except when some woman's face or voice reminded him fleetingly of his liking for Alicia Clare. Until last year, for that liking's sake and because his wandering convalescent's freedom was beginning to seem like being lost in space, he had called again at Martlets, and had found Alicia newly widowed, Marco a fraught adolescent half rebellious and half obsessed with duty, the two younger children in different ways disturbed. And somehow he had stayed, tied by threads of old association and new habit. 'Oh, don't go away,' Alicia said once, down-to-earth as a factory foreman; 'I should be sad.' 'You int so much in demand, booy,' said Marco, 'that you can't spare some time for us.' 'I *love* Crispin,' Mikey would enthuse, rubbing his cheek against the cousinly bristles; while Lucy, less extrovert, would sometimes beg: 'Crispin, do please take Mummy out for a drink, she's being just awful.'

A high red wall surrounded the house, which stood end-on to the road, showing motorists only a blank gable and some trees. But to the pedestrian the gates disclosed a pleasingly geometrical vista, every window of the black-and-white-house balancing every other window, every beam every other beam, the whole seeming, because of its insistent verticals, longer than it was. Precisely midway in the façade was the big door, before which many a Tudor wagon must have drawn up to receive bales from the loft two stories above. Around the doorway, already elaborately carved, the Melfords, framing the frame, had displayed numbers of martlets. 'I'll bet,' Mark Clare said, 'those people had a martlet-shaped swimming pool.'

The snowy garden, tree-shadowed, had turned blue. Clare beat on the oak door. Inside, responding swiftly as a dog, Mikey shouted.

When the door opened the glow of the hall burst out across the snow. In the great brick fireplace logs were blazing. It was a large room, normally almost bare but for a carved settle, and the barbaric light danced in every corner. The round shade of an oil-lamp on a card-table before the chimney looked by contrast very pallid.

'Do be quick,' Lucy said, and the heavy door banged behind him the moment he stepped forward. She was urgent for his coat. '*Isn't* it perishing? Poor you, you're all pink and purple.'

Lucy was ten. She was wearing, if not her school uniform, something scarcely distinct. Clare often thought of her, between quotation marks, as a good little body; obliging, cheerful, self-effacing. But while thinking so, he sometimes wondered whether a change might not come with adolescence; whether she would not later find herself deserving of more of her own attention. For the moment, though, she fitted perfectly the space alloted to her, as the family's one daughter placed between two widely separated, not at all self-effacing males.

The younger of the males put his hand in Clare's in a proprietorial way and led him nearer the fire. Mikey was six. He was proprietorial about several people, particularly Clare and Marco.

Amabel was seated at the table, her back towards them, her fair head bent. Clare wondered what absorbed her, and peeped

10

over her shoulder. In front of her, arranged in a cross, were five Tarot cards.

'Good lord,' he said. 'Where do you get such things?'

Amabel, roused, looked round at him and smiled. Amabel was seven. Her fair hair was very light, and her eyes a misty confusion of hazel and green. With her fragile features, her tiny voice, the faint reserve which never left her, there was something unearthly about Amabel. Mark addressed her as 'Tinkerbell'.

A *wicked pack of cards* came floating into Clare's mind as he stared down. On the left was the Hanged Man, looking quite happy. 'I didn't know they were still made.'

'Marco got them in London,' Lucy said. 'They tell your fortune somehow.'

'Crispin,' said Amabel, in her Tinkerbell voice.

'Hullo, my changeling.'

'You made a mistake,' said Amabel, 'and there's going to be trouble, but you'll get out of it and be very happy. But you will need to be much bolder in love.'

Truly astonished, 'You are the most extraordinary kid,' Clare exclaimed. But then all three children burst out laughing, and he understood why Amabel had been so preoccupied when he came in.

'She's practised it,' Lucy let on. 'She learned that one by heart, out of the little book.'

'Are we going to do the other thing now?' asked Mikey. 'I'll tell Marco.' He scampered across the room and bawled up the stairs: 'Crispin's here.'

A side door opened, and Alicia came in wheeling a trolley. 'I thought so,' she said at the sight of Clare. 'How nice and punctual you are. Happy New Year.' He hesitated, then gave her a peck on the cheek. Hardly acknowledging that, she stood examining the glowing hall. 'Marco's big blaze was a picturesque idea, but where is there to sit or to put things down?'

'In the Middle Ages,' Lucy said, 'everything happened in the hall.'

'I shouldn't be a bit surprised,' said Alicia primly.

11

The fire brought out red glints in her hair, which was arranged in what Clare took to be a pageboy style, at least a style recalling the Duc de Berry's pageboys. The light suited her skin. She looked handsome and young. Suddenly she gave him the smile which she had absently forgotten, and Clare's heart went out to her. She was still the ally who had amused him when, unhappy with strangeness of the country which was supposed to be his homeland, he had shivered in that house. 'Amabel,' she said, 'I'm going to have to use that table, I'm sorry. Oh, those beastly cards, I hate them. Did you know they're still making them, Crispin? – or making them again. Marco says all that mad old ladies' stuff is coming back.'

'I should have thought they would interest you,' Clare said. 'Visually, I mean.' He cut the stack which Amabel had put aside, and gazed upon the Devil. 'Odd, that. I've never seen a chap in tights that had, as you might say, compartments.'

'Marco's idea,' Alicia said, 'was to inspire me to make money. He thought I might design a pack. He's sure fortunes are going to be made out of anything that's irrational.'

Mark Clare, very tall, came down the narrow shadowed stairs into the light, his nineteen-year-old body seeming to be made up largely of blue denim legs. In his recent-schoolboy's mumble, he said: 'Happy birthday, Cris.'

'Have you had a birthday since Christmas?' said Alicia. 'How does he know that when I don't?'

'In the summer,' Mark said, 'we were doing some astrology. Just fooling about, you know. Cris is complicated because he was born in the southern hemisphere. Good practice.'

'If my father could hear his grandson –' Alicia began.

'He'd whip out my nuciform sac,' Mark said, 'the old horse-doctor. Intelligence is curiosity, Ma.'

'Personally, I'd sooner be a cabbage,' said Alicia, 'than a crackpot. Cabbages have the respect of their neighbours.'

'Did Marco say it's your birthday?' Mikey barged in.

'Not today,' Clare said. 'The day before yesterday.'

'How old are you?' demanded the child, as if suspicious of that answer. He stood four-square in the baronial room, looking up with round blue eyes under his cap of straight, rope-coloured hair. Mikey could be intensely, bullyingly masculine.

'Twenty-five.'

Amabel, with a flimsy booklet in her hand, began to make a calculation. 'Two and five is seven. Seven is the Chariot. That's a very good card, Crispin. Success, health and long life.'

'She's eerie,' Alicia observed aside. 'Lovely to look at, and super-intelligent, but eerie.'

'I just hope she's reliable,' said Clare.

'Mummy, how old are you?' Mikey wanted to know.

'As old as her tongue and older than her teeth,' Mark said.

'Don't be stupid,' his little brother said squashingly. 'How old, Mummy?'

'As old as − ' said Alicia, reflecting; 'as old as Senator Kennedy.'

'President Kennedy,' Lucy said.

'No, Clever Clogs,' Alicia said, 'Senator. He hasn't been inaugurated yet.'

'Another number seven,' said Clare. 'Success, health and long life.'

'*How old?*' Mikey insisted, a tantrum brewing in his voice.

'Sixty-one,' Mark said. 'Poor old boot, she shouldn't be standing about. Come and park your rheumatics on the settle, gal.'

They lined up on the settle, the three adults and Mikey, like birds on a wire. When Lucy and Amabel had poured the tea and handed sandwiches they joined them. There was plenty of hard shiny room, but the settle did not make for conversation. Mark, at one end, leaned forward and said to Clare, at the other: ''Scuse me, squire, is this the line for Hammersmith?'

'I wondered what was missing,' Alicia said. 'No advertisements to read.'

The adults made do instead with the flames which were mounting, revived, about a new pile of long logs. But the children were restless, hurried in their courtesies with sugar or cake. At length Alicia said: 'All right, Lucy. Get out that silly game, as your heart is set on it.'

13

Instantly the table was cleared, and the board was conjured from somewhere by Amabel. Mikey seemed to have very precise ideas about the placing of the chairs. Lucy's final touches were even more precise, measurable in millimetres.

'Now, Crispin,' said Mikey, standing lackey-like by a chair.

Clare rose, but hesitated. 'Who is the other person? Amabel?'

'I think,' Lucy said, 'it's best if you start with someone who's really bad at it. That means Marco.'

Mark, getting up, slouched to another chair, collapsed his long legs and grinned at Clare. 'One does feel a charley,' he said. Confronted by him, Clare noted that a term of university had already matured and fined down his face, with its sharply angled jaw. He seemed likely to inherit a share of Alicia's faintly pre-Raphaelite looks.

'What do we do?' Clare asked him.

'Well,' Mark said, 'we each put a finger on the little tea-trolley thing, and wait. Thank you, Mikey.' For Mikey had also precise ideas about the placing of their fingers.

'I'm waiting,' Clare said. And went on waiting. Because there was nothing else to look at, they looked at one another, which began to get on their nerves.

From the settle, Alicia remarked: 'You two have the most fed-up expressions I've ever seen on you.'

'I just don't find Cris all that interesting,' said Mark. 'I mean, he's normal – he's got a mouth-shaped mouth and a nose-shaped nose. But there's nothing you want to linger over.'

'I'm keeping my mind occupied,' Clare said, 'by counting the acne.'

'Oh you sod,' Mark muttered.

'Marco,' said Lucy, patiently, 'you ought to say something to it.'

Mark cleared his throat. Then he said in a Goon Show voice: 'Hullo, folks, hullo, folks, calling all folks. Is there anyone there?'

Immediately the little wheeled indicator came to life. It said, firmly and emphatically: NO.

'Marco!' yelled Mikey, with rage.

'You fraud, Marco,' Lucy said. 'Oh well, no harm done, I suppose. Let Amabel have your chair now, see what she can do with Crispin.' Mark's long shape reared up, shadowing the table, and almost at once Clare saw the uncanny child materialize in the place opposite him.

Her finger was tiny. To see his own near it made Clare feel like a caveman, and none too clean.

She said: 'Will you ask the questions, Crispin?'

'No,' he said, 'you do it, you're practised.'

The little voice, so oddly precise, asked: 'Is anybody there?' And with no great speed, but effortlessly and inevitably, the board answered: YES.

'Is the person there,' Amabel asked, 'who wanted to speak to Crispin?'

YES.

'What is your name?'

The board spelled out three letters, then stopped. M–A–L.

'*Mal*,' said Mark. 'Cris, you've hit the jackpot. *Mal*. I should think that was something slow and terminal.'

'Marco, belt up,' said his mother quietly. 'It's not his fortune, it's a name.' She left the settle and came to stand with the others around the card-table.

The message had seemed to come to an end, but with a jerk the indicator darted towards another letter.

'E,' said Lucy, scribbling on the pad in her hand.

All at once the thing was full of purpose; it swooped across the board. What it wrote meant nothing to Clare, yet he was somehow alarmed by its assurance. When it was still he looked round at Lucy.

'Any sense?' he asked her.

She frowned over the pad. 'Not that I can see. Here, you look.' She tore off a sheet and laid it beside him.

At first it was a jumble. Then the letters separated into words. 'Good God,' he said.

A log fell, and the light flared around the edges of Amabel's hair, shadowing her pointed face.

He pushed the paper towards her. 'Do you understand that?'

For a moment she gazed at him, with her ambiguously coloured, very beautiful eyes. Then she studied the paper, wrinkling her forehead under the pale hair.

'This isn't anything,' she said, 'is it? It isn't English.'

'Could you pronounce it?'

'Of course not.'

'It's Latin,' Clare said. 'You don't know any Latin, do you?'

She only laughed at the question.

'Mark – could you read it?'

'I was good at Latin once,' Alicia said, 'let me try.' She reached for the paper, but Mark had taken it. Standing together, flame outlining them, they turned so that the firelight fell full on the sheet.

'Oh,' said Alicia after a moment, 'I've no patience with this sort of thing.' She relinquished it to her son. 'It's gibberish.'

'If it's Latin,' Mark said, less confidently, 'Cardinal Wolsey wasted our money on educating me.'

'It splits up into words,' Clare said. 'Can you see?'

'His Latin was always terrible,' said Alicia. 'Even worse than Lucy's writing. Tell us what you think it is.'

Clare said: 'The first word is a name. It says: "*Malekin me vocitabam*." It means: "I used to call myself Malkin." '

All the time he was watching Amabel's face, which showed no surprise or interest. 'Ask her,' he said, 'another question, Tinkerbell.'

'*Her?*' repeated the child, and the lovely eyes changed just a shade.

Clare explained: 'She's a little girl. Use her name to her. It's Malkin, remember.'

Amabel bent her head and spoke into the centre of the board. Her tone was gentle. 'Your name is Malkin?'

The board said: YES.

'Where do you live, Malkin?'

16

The board spelled out a rapid word. Lucy tore off a sheet of her pad and slapped it on the table.

'*Suthfolke*,' Mark read. 'Is that supposed to be Suffolk?'

'*I* can spell Suffolk,' Mikey let everyone know.

'She's very young,' Clare excused. 'Amabel, ask her where she was born.'

Amabel, imperturbable, asked in her fairy television presenter's voice: 'Where were you born, Malkin?'

This time the board was not so fast that Clare could not follow. His finger tensed and relaxed as each expected letter came. He knew what would be on the sheet which Lucy planked before him.

'*Lanaham?*' said Mark, doubtfully. 'There's no such place. Not in Suthfolke.'

'She means Lavenham,' said Clare.

Mark revolted. 'Oh, come off it, Cris. What gives you the right to twist any jumble of words that crops up into what you want it to look like?'

Clare was very calm, indeed cold. 'She was born in the twelfth century. That's how they wrote it then.'

He was not much aware of the others, he was so intent on Amabel's supernatural, seven-year-old beauty.

'I refuse,' Alicia said, 'to listen to any more of this rubbish.' She began to load tea-things noisily on to the trolley.

Mikey asked: 'How old is Malkin?'

'You heard the expert,' Mark said. 'Eight hundred odd.'

'Then she's dead.'

'I reckon. Probably the Minister for Pensions shot her.'

'I don't think she is dead,' said Clare. 'I don't think she ever died or got any older.'

'What a lovely person.' Mark was enthusiastic. 'Sort of like Lucille Ball.'

Clare grew aware of Amabel's grave little face turned full on him. She said: 'Crispin, we haven't finished.'

'No?' he said. 'Has she got a message?'

'I don't know. You speak now.'

He concentrated on his forefinger, which had coaldust in

17

the nail. He heard Alicia's trolley rattle away, and a bang of the door. 'Malkin — are you still there?'

YES.

'Is there something you want to tell me?'

NO.

'Is there somebody else who wants to speak to me?'

YES.

'What is the message?'

The letters came slowly, hesitantly. He saw each one approach, with dread. GALA BU KU SAKAPU.

Two logs fell in, in a flurry of sparks and flame. The fever struck him in an instant. Every tendon was drawn tight, as at the worst times.

The thing went on writing. A SISU.

He cried out: '*Ku sasòpa*! *Bogwo a sakapu. Avei tau yoku? Amyagam?*'

The board wrote: KULISAPINI.

He stood up, and his chair fell to the floor. He was falling after it, but Mark's bony body stopped him. Later he was half sprawled on the settle, his face against Mark's pullover. There was a hot hand on his forehead.

'*A katoulo*,' he muttered. '*A katoulo sitana. Igau bi bwoina. O, kagu toki, so.*'

'*Lu ku kaliga*,' Mark murmured. Or so he thought for a moment. But Mark had said: 'You fainted.'

'*E*,' he agreed. 'My head fainted.'

'My fault. It's much too hot in here.'

'*I livala* — ' Clare began.

'We don't understand that language.'

'It said it was me.'

'What did?'

'That thing. It said its name was Kulisapini. That's my name. It said: "You'll never escape." It said: "I'm still here." It means I died there.'

'Easy, easy,' Mark said, rocking him. 'It was just the heat. Now take it quietly. You know, you're frightening the horses, so to speak.'

18

Through his self-absorption Clare felt the guilt of his lapse, and looked at the children. Amabel still sat at the card-table, her back to the fire. She watched him with the detachment of a robin. But Lucy's inexpressive face, in spite of herself, had taken on expression, and Clare could read it. Lucy knew that adults, the most familiar and loved and irreplaceable of them, might faint and take to their beds and die. And at his very knee, so that he had to look down, was Mikey. He could not think how to atone for Mikey's wonder and terror.

'Crispin?' Mikey said. It was a question, faint as a breeze. A midget hand reached out and took a handful of Clare's trouser-leg, and gently tugged at it. 'Crispin, what's the matter?'

'Nothing, Mikey,' Clare said. 'I just came over funny.' The small face revealed too much: Mikey had meant it when he said: 'I love Crispin.' He did love the real Crispin; not the misadventure being dealt with by his brother.

'Crispin passed out,' Mark said. 'It happens.'

All at once Mikey's face was full of enlightenment. 'Oh,' he exclaimed, 'is he drunk?'

The feeling of Mark laughing against him made Clare laugh too. Even Lucy, considering what would be for the best, willed a smile. 'Yes,' Clare said. 'It happens.'

'Marco was drunk last night,' said Mikey, reassured. 'He went to sleep in the kitchen.'

'Flippin' hell,' Mark muttered. 'As Genghis Khan said, the basis of the police state is the family.'

'You don't smell drunk,' said Mikey, critically.

'That,' said Mark, 'is going to be attended to. What do you say, Cris? It would cheer Lucy up to be doing the St Bernard thing with a whisky bottle.'

The Tarot cards which the children had placed on the settle for tidiness had fallen and were scattered over the floor, face-down except for one. By Mikey's foot, which must have kicked it, lay the Hanged Man. Calm and content, hands behind his back, he dangled. Clare, leaning forward, his elbows on his knees, tried to make sense of it.

19

Lucy had come nearer. 'Would you like that, Crispin? A glass of whisky, or something?'

'No, nothing, thanks,' he said, absently. 'This card is very odd.'

Mark, beside him, leaned to look. 'Odder than the rest?'

'It's the wrong way up in every kind of way. He must be upside down, because of his hair. But that doesn't look like a gibbet. He seems to be hanging from the earth, between two trees.'

Mark said: 'You're not making it any clearer to me.'

'Oh well, these things don't set out to be scrutable,' Clare admitted. 'I just had a thought about what it might have been, originally. I suppose there's nothing in it, but it reminded me of things I've been reading lately. Things they thought they knew, in the Middle Ages, about the Antipodes and their land.'

'Oh-ah,' said Mark, abstracted. He had begun to hum fragments of a tune. 'Well, it's an idea.'

'Your mother hasn't come back. Do you think she's fed up with our games?'

'You go and ask her,' Mark suggested. 'You know where she'll be.'

Through the dark rooms of the old house, which had become again so familiar, Clare made his way to the newer, eighteenth-century wing. That was the part which Alicia preferred, and he found her in the high whitewashed kitchen, where he was used to seeing her, straightbacked in a basket-chair in front of the stove. She acknowledged him with her quick smile.

'We're all abject for boring you,' he said. 'The seance is over now.'

'I wasn't avoiding it,' she said. 'I suddenly noticed Mikey's gloves and thought I must mend them. Sit there, and make some adult conversation.'

'I can't think what about,' he said. 'It's a quiet life I lead.'

Alicia said: 'Sometimes I envy you that cottage. If I lived there, alone, I'd paint and paint.'

20

'Are you working on something?'

'I hope. Oh, but one does let oneself down. Yesterday it was exciting. Today it looks like a Christmas card.'

'That means snow,' he said. 'You like white, don't you?' He thought that that was why the tall pale room, with its plain wood and plain crockery, seemed especially her place, after the firelit antiquity of the hall.

She finished a darn and put the small glove down. 'I hope I didn't seem a killjoy over the ouija board. But it does annoy me. It was you, of course, who were writing the Latin.'

'I think that's true,' he said, 'but I don't understand. I didn't fake it. Nor did Amabel. She was somehow getting messages from me. Unnerving child.'

Alicia said compassionately: 'If you find that, it's probably to do with her home life. I think that's not much fun.'

'I can't believe in Amabel's home life. I imagine her living with a witch, and going home to a hollow tree. I can't believe in her name. Anyone called Amabel ought to be a hundred and twenty years old, with a cameo brooch.'

'Actually, she lives in a house which is rather grand. Her father is very rich. And also very respectable. I deduce that from the fact that he has custody.'

'I see,' Clare said. 'Is she the only one?'

'Oh, doesn't it show? I think she's really awfully lonely. And intensely observant of people who are not.'

'That's what I remembered,' Clare said: 'your knowing way with waifs and strays.'

She faintly smiled, but he felt that she too was reassured by what she provided for others. The soberly ticking cottage clock, the jar of dried honesty and achillea, the ropes of onions hanging from a high beam, were all tributes to rural restfulness in another time.

'It's snowing again,' she remarked, and at the thought moved her chair nearer the stove. 'I noticed when I drew the curtains. Isn't it miserably cold down there? You ought to give a thought to pneumonia, as you're not used to it.'

'It's bracing,' he said. 'Indoors and out. I feel pretty fit on it.'

'I suppose those malaria things,' she said, 'can't survive it. Oh, did Marco tell you what the Indian said to his lecturer? No? Well, this man who lectures Marco felt sorry for the dark-looking people he saw freezing in the London streets, and he said so to this Indian. And the Indian said: "Oh, good gracious me, sir. When you pass us shivering at a bus-stop, you are not to be feeling sorry for us. You are to be saying to yourself: For the first time in their lives they are losing their amoebic dysentery."'

She leaned forward and, reaching down, rattled with something which Clare believed was called a riddle. When that sound stopped, he thought he could hear a distant guitar.

'Marco,' noted Alicia. 'In his room. Isn't it silent today? I haven't heard one car go past.'

Though it was faint, Clare thought he recognized what the guitar was playing as something by Bach, something favoured by Segovia.

'Things go fairly well,' he said, 'with Marco, so I gather.'

'I suppose they do,' Alicia said. 'It's rather soon to tell.'

He thought he knew what she had been thinking about, sitting alone in the kitchen, but the time had probably passed for speaking of it. Twelve months before, Charles Clare had not yet been aware of his illness. He guessed that Alicia, at the first turn of the year without him, had willed herself to think only forwards.

Abruptly she asked: 'Is the sun over the yardarm?' and craned her neck to see his watch. 'Oh good. Now I shall have one cigarette and two gins.'

'What a crazy expression,' Clare said, 'to use in this climate and weather. To me it means O.P. rum with coconut-milk, and that sort of purple light that comes just before dark.'

'I'm sorry to say,' remarked Alicia, 'that I don't know Worthing.'

He got up, ready to open the door for her, but she still sat in the basketwork chair. She asked: 'Have you found anything to do yet, Cris?'

'Oh – yes and no. I usually have my frostbitten nose in a book.'

'That old Latin, still? Will anything come of it?'

'I don't know,' he said. 'There's something I want to do, but I don't see how. Like you with your painting, I find that I let myself down. Though you know you don't, Lissa.'

'It is rather cheering,' she said, 'to push on anyway. Who was it who believed in acting "As If"?'

'Camus,' he said, 'I think. Yes, I do know the cheer of pushing on. Out there,' he explained, suddenly diffident, 'I used to do a lot of writing. I thought I might forget the language otherwise.'

He saw that she approved, but exactly as she approved of Mark's new interest in music, on principle. 'It is odd,' she said, 'to think of a Clare swotting away at his Latin down in The Hole. Oh, I've remembered something. Do you think you could face a game of Monopoly with the children?'

'I suppose I could,' he said. 'But what a jump, from spooks to real estate.'

'How quickly they jump from anything to anything. I find the adaptability of children rather inhuman. Do you know that last year little Amabel was flown all the way to Hong Kong, and couldn't remember afterwards seeing anything that was worth mentioning.' She rose from the creaking chair, and put away her needles and wool in a drawer.

On the high mantelshelf, level with his eye, Clare noticed a photograph taken in the garden in late summer. Mikey was grimacing at the photographer, Lucy was selfconsciously sensible. On the grass several yards of Mark were disposed, huge feet towards the camera. Alicia, in a headscarf, was glancing aside at Clare himself, whose face was white and hollow-eyed. He thought: One would say that man was terrified.

Alicia said, watching him: 'Sometimes you did look like that. Not now, though. Much more healthy and cabbage-like now.' She opened the door, and the guitar grew louder. He followed her out, into the older, darker house, in which there were distant sounds of Mikey throwing a tantrum.

On the road the new snow lay powdery and creaking. 'This is a bit better,' said Mark. 'I went flat on my back here last night.' He stamped his heavy boots and swung his long arms, looking massive and dark in the white-gleaming night.

Ahead the red curtains of the Shoulder of Mutton glowed like coals. A light but bitter breeze had risen, and the pub sign creaked a little.

'Goo-to-hell, booy,' Mark shivered, 'thass a lazy old wind.'

'Why "lazy"?' Clare asked.

'That don't want to goo round you, that just goo through.'

As they reached the pub door it opened and a girl came out, almost colliding with Mark, who stepped clumsily aside, scattering snow. She was a slight girl, whose hair, lit from behind, shone very fair.

'Hullo there,' Mark said. 'Happy New Year.'

The girl's eyes, as well as Clare could see, were green or blue. She paid no attention to Mark, but looked past him at the night, then stepped forward and walked away across the snow.

'Could you say,' Clare asked, enjoying Mark's discomfited face, 'that someone had lazy eyes? Hers certainly went straight through you.'

'Foreign bitch,' Mark muttered. 'All right, we haven't been introduced, but that's no reason for her to treat me as if I was a flasher.' He pushed the heavy curtain aside, and Clare, following, banged the door.

The long bar was full of wood-smoke and tobacco-smoke, trapped between the low ceiling and the red-quarried floor. Clare, as he took his place beside Mark in front of the leaping fire, felt his eyes immediately and as usual begin to smart. While Mark acknowledged the automatic greetings, he asked curiously: 'Who was she?'

'Ah,' Mark said. 'Fancied her, did you?'

'I hardly saw her. She looked interesting.'

24

'She's one of Lady Munby's au pairs. They come and go. From Scandinavia and thereabouts. Usually their English is more theory than practice. I suppose she didn't want to get into a conversation she couldn't understand.'

Clare wondered why she had been there at all, in a bar where so many spoke a dialect which baffled Londoners. That male and smoky place was no setting for her ethereal blondeness.

A gypsy-looking boy in a woollen cap, who was practising darts by himself, turned at the board and called to Mark: 'Sudbury!' Mark made a vaguely rude gesture at him, and moved on towards the bar.

'What does that mean?' Clare wondered.

'Sudbury? It means you're keeping the fire off everyone else. No one knows why.'

Behind the bar the landlord nodded: 'Evening, Mark, Cris,' and reached under the counter for two pint pots. Filling one at a tap, he asked as an afterthought: 'Bitter?' and without waiting for an answer went on: 'Still snowing?'

'Sky's clearing,' Mark said. 'Peter, do you know that girl's name?'

The landlord set down one pot and started on the second. 'What girl is that?'

'The blonde bird. The foreign one.'

The landlord, in a bright yellow cardigan which was clearly a Christmas present, was solid, bald and slow. 'Blonde bird,' he said to himself, pondering. 'Oh-ah. Just now went out. First time I sin her.'

'It's mine,' Clare said, putting his money down. 'Good health, Marco.'

'Cheers, Crissie,' said Mark. 'By the way, I'm called Mark outside the nest.'

'She come in with Jim,' the landlord said. 'She only stay five minutes.'

Clare followed his gesture to see which Jim he meant, and noticed the large man sitting alone at one end of the bar. Reading the clues of the man's face and coat and short hair, he concluded that Jim was American. He said to the landlord:

'Air Force?' and was then abashed to find that the stranger had turned his head and was looking back at him. To break contact he raised his pot and squinted into it.

'No,' Peter said; 'tourist. We put him up just before Christmas. Nice chap, Jim. Not much to say for himself, for a Yank.'

Mark, who had dreams of California and wild freedoms, gave the Yank an interested glance, but found him too old to matter. In a tactful movement his eye travelled on to the dart-board, and watched the gypsy-looking boy, with much preparation, plant three darts in it. Mark said loudly: 'Rubbish.'

The dark youth turned and looked at him, impassive, but with humour in his long-cut eyes. He said: 'Should you care to make a spectacle of yourself, dear boy?'

'Mind if I leave you alone for a while, Cris?' Mark asked. And as Clare, drinking, gave an assenting shrug, he took the darts which the landlord handed him from behind the bar and went to join the boy in the knitted cap.

'Robin will give him the brush and have a pint off him,' Peter said. 'He int very sharp, young Mark.' His straying eye took in some slight gesture from the American, and he wandered away to the other end of the bar.

Clare, studying a beermat, listened to the light thud of darts, the click of dominoes on a table behind him. A dart thunked into wood, then fell to the floor, and one of the domino-players called sardonically: 'Lovely arrers, Mark.'

The American, Clare noticed, was drinking double whiskies, which in a public bar in Swainstead made him exotic.

He felt a light tug at his trouser-leg, reminding him of Mikey, and looking down met the stare of a black kitten. Its mouth moved in a silent mew. He wondered what impossible thing it could expect from him, with eyes so indecipherable and intent.

The domino-player explained in the same slow voice: 'What she want, Cris, is she want you to buy a packet of crisps.' At the sound of his name he swung round, and saw John with his

26

face again downturned over his hand of tiles. Somehow he always wanted to laugh at the sight of John, the type of the young yokel from nineteenth-century melodrama. His hair, cut pudding-basin fashion, was like frost-bitten grass. From under his fringe, small round blue eyes, already netted in weather-lines, looked up with the slyness of purest innocence. The prototype of John had always thought itself a shrewd sort of chap, even as it went like a lamb to the chair of Sweeney Todd.

He was not used to seeing John away from the farm, and was surprised to recognize in the back of the other domino-player John's older and very taciturn work-mate Roger. In the summer, so it had seemed to Clare, they must have spent almost every waking hour together. Perhaps such habits became necessities. Roger, with a wrench of his black head, growled: 'How do, Cris,' and went back to studying his tiles.

The robust, canary-breasted landlord returned, and said: 'Jim say would you like a drink?' He seemed embarrassed by the message.

'But I don't know him,' Clare said. 'Why me? Anyway, I'm not ready.'

The landlord, too, was uneasy about such foreign manners. 'I just mentioned to him you was interested in the same kind of things.'

Not knowing what the things were, Clare looked for a clue to the American himself, and seeing in the other man's face an expectation, picked up his beer and walked to where he sat. At his approach the American turned on his stool, and seemed with a movement of his eyes to suggest another stool, which Clare as silently took.

'Peter,' said the American, at length, 'tells me you're an antiquarian.'

The word struck Clare as strange, perhaps because it was presented as coming from the landlord's mouth. 'He told me,' he said, 'that you were a tourist. So am I, more or less.'

The American sipped his whisky. 'You're called Cris.'

'Yes. You're called Jim.'

27

'Right.' The American seemed to consider the idea of shaking hands, and to drop it. 'Could I buy you a drink?'

'Not now, thanks,' Clare said. 'What do you do, as a tourist?'

'I poke around in churches,' the American said. 'Like you, I hear.'

'Yes, I've done a bit of that,' Clare admitted. He remained wary of the stranger, who would sooner or later ask some question difficult to answer.

In the room behind them Mark burst out: 'What the hell's the matter with me?' and Robin said: 'You need a white stick and a dog, that's what's the matter.'

'It's great,' the American said; 'the accent.'

'I like it,' Clare agreed, growing easier with him. 'Perhaps that's atavism. My people must have spoken pretty broad at one time.'

'But not now,' the American supposed.

'We're extinct. Well, nearly. I've two or three distant cousins. That beanpole playing darts so badly is one.'

On Mark's half of the board, virgin of any score, Robin was chalking the outline of a whitewash brush, incomplete.

'I guess we're extinct, too,' the American said, 'in Europe. Not that I looked very hard when I was in Brittany.' As Clare put interest into his face, the man explained: 'I'm French-Canadian, from Maine. My name's Jacques Maunoir.'

For friendliness, Clare said: 'Crispin Clare,' and for civility they did shake hands after all.

'Crispin,' the big man said thoughtfully. 'Crispin Clare. I know that name.'

'I've a headstone in the churchyard,' Clare said. 'It even has my address on it.'

'The Hole,' Jim Maunoir remembered. 'Does it make you laugh, too?'

'It did,' Clare said. 'Not that I often hear it, except from old people.'

A groan came from Mark as Robin speared his last double.

'Shot, sir!' he congratulated hollowly. 'Nice arrow, boy. Jammy prat.'

'The beanpole lost,' deduced Jim Maunoir.

'Didn't even score,' Clare confirmed. 'Obviously you've poked around the church here.'

'I did a brass-rubbing,' Maunoir said, 'as well as I could with my hands frozen. Were you here before that girl went out?'

'We passed her,' Clare said. The kitten was tugging at Maunoir's leg, and the two of them were staring at one another.

'Why I asked,' Maunoir said, 'was because I met her in the church. Well, it wasn't a meeting, but we were both there. And tonight I passed her on the road, a mile outside the village, tramping along through the snow. So I offered her a ride, and after that a drink to thaw her out. She came in just to please me, that was made clear, but she wouldn't settle. She was like a bird. Do you know her?'

'No,' Clare said. 'Nobody seems to know her. She's foreign, isn't she?'

'Is she?' Maunoir said, surprised. 'She could be. She surely doesn't talk a lot. She has some kind of accent, but I picked her for a local girl.'

'Perhaps she is,' Clare said. 'Probably Mark mixed her up with someone else.'

'A really strange kind of girl,' said Maunoir, reliving it. 'I mean, yes and no were quite long speeches. And she looks at you. This cat made me think of her. She looks at you like that, and her eyes are green.'

Imagining the scene, Clare realized what it was about Maunoir that, by striking him as slightly out of key, appealed to his sympathies. The American seemed to be in his early thirties, and of the type from which Hollywood drew its football heroes. His frame was large, his hair cropped, and his strong and open face potentially stern. At variance with every-thing else, his eyes were somehow undefended. If the blonde girl had stared at him like the kitten, it would have been

29

with a kind of manly wistfulness that he looked back at her.

A hand clamped on Clare's shoulder, and Mark said: 'Lend me half a crown, mate. I've enough for your pint, but I owe Robin one.'

Clare rummaged in his jacket pocket and found a crumpled note. 'Here, have ten bob,' he said. 'And I don't need a drink.'

'You've got one,' Mark said, 'in the stable,' and he went back to Robin.

Maunoir said: 'If your family's extinct, it won't lie down. That was done like a brother. On his side, I mean.'

Clare said: 'You sound like a brother.'

'Oh yeah,' the big man said, 'there's a whole bunch of Maunoirs where I came from.' Suddenly he seemed to have something faintly saddening on his mind. 'Even the younger ones always figure I need a dollar.'

'What do you do?' Clare asked. 'Sorry, I take back that question. Only, I wondered whether you might be something interesting, like a starving genius.'

'No, sir,' Maunoir said, and flashed his candid smile (his Joe College smile, thought Clare, who had been a film-goer in his student days), which his light-coloured eyes contradicted by seeming to be shadowed over. 'All I am is a retired teacher.'

'Retired?'

'Temporarily retired. This fall I took off.'

Clare wondered, because of the shadowy sadness, about divorce, or widowerhood, or even a scandal involving a pupil. But he wanted no more information about Jim Maunoir, who would surely expect some return.

And Maunoir expected already. 'You wouldn't be a starving genius yourself?'

'Shut up about starving,' Clare said. 'No, I'm –'. He saw that a brief dash would do it best. 'I'm also retired. I was a very raw anthropologist, working for one of the colonial governments. About eighteen months ago I was bowled over by tropical diseases, some way from a doctor. I took leave, but it turned into resignation.'

He began to notice a change in Maunoir's demeanour, a change which made him more familiar, though Clare could not think why. It was partly that he listened and looked so intently.

'You people are casual about that word "colonial",' he remarked.

'Just then,' Clare said shortly, 'I used it correctly.' At once he regretted the shortness, though it had made no impression on Maunoir's rather commanding, grave face. 'But if you mean I'm a relic of the past, I admit it. I am.' It ocurred to him that a deluge of personal details would be likely to kill unwanted questions. I was born in South Africa, of a New Zealand mother and a father born in India. My mother and I sat out the war in New Zealand. After that, my father was in Malaya, and I went to boarding school in Australia. Then he was in Kenya, and I went to school in Devon. The end of the Empire was pretty confusing to families like mine.'

He had been fiddling with his pint-pot, printing circle on circle with a little beer which he had slopped. When he looked up, he understood with sudden, amazing clarity the expression of Jim Maunoir. What he had taken for a kind of wistfulness was a kind of bargaining. The eyes said: In return for what I admit of the sadness of myself, have confidence that I won't fail to understand you.

Clare could not take his own eyes off the man. 'You're a priest.'

Maunoir did not answer, and his face did not change.

Something happened inside Clare's head, something which had happened before. It was as though his brain fell backwards a short way. Afterwards, he asked: 'Who sent you?'

Maunoir gave his Joe College smile, but his eyes were the same. He said: 'What a question, Cris.'

'Oh, I thought it was over,' Clare muttered, in despair. 'The priests. The psychotherapists. I thought it was all over now.'

Maunoir asked: 'Are people sent here often, Cris?'

'Not here,' Clare said. 'Not in this country. Oh Jesus, I don't want it spoiled in this country.'

'Listen,' Maunoir said. 'No, look at me, Crispin.' His shadowed eyes were offered like a vow. 'No one will be sent to you in this country. And I am not a priest.'

'No?' said Clare, doubting. 'Would you lie to me, Jim?'

'I was a Jesuit,' Maunoir said. 'I'm not one now.'

Clare put his head down, and breathed deep. He looked at the toes of his Wellingtons among the fag-ends. He started to laugh.

'What's the joke?' Maunoir asked.

'I'm paranoid,' Clare said, still laughing. 'Paranoid. It *is* a joke.'

Maunoir said genially: 'It wouldn't take much to convince me you were psychic. *Non psycho sed psychico.* A fatherly funny. Here comes the beer from your cousin. Sit up straight now and drink it like a man.'

Clare pushed aside his emptied pot and looked at the circles on circles stamped in drying beer over the shining wood of the bar. So inside atoms. So in all space. The everlasting terror of a process without term.

'How did you know?' asked Maunoir, his glass at his mouth.

'I notice things. I'm a trained voyeur. Like you, Jim.'

'Try again,' invited Maunoir. 'That hardly got through my hair shirt.'

Saluting Mark, drinking Mark's beer, Clare thought to ask: 'What does it feel like, for you?'

'Maybe you know,' said Maunoir. 'It feels like being lost in the woods.'

'Yes,' Clare said. 'Yes, I do know.' He thought of his dream, of how he had looked up out of his hole, his pit, his wolf-pit, and seen the foreign leaves, which had formed themselves into a face, invulnerably amused.

Jim Maunoir had grown remote, gazing beyond Clare's shoulder. His eyes were clouded over. He had the mouth of a good little boy, the priest's favourite.

Clare thought of Alicia's voice. He said: 'Don't go away, Jim; I should be sad.'

Walking with Clare to the top of Hole Lane, Mark said: 'I'm glad we went out and met Jim. He's such a young sort of bloke for his age. Some of the things he says are really funny.'

Mark sounded a little elevated. While Clare had been playing dominoes with John, Jim Maunoir must have poured several whiskies into him.

'The accent,' Clare said, 'helps him to be funny.' He himself had felt the charm of Maunoir's laconic manner when he relaxed, the stylishness of what Clare thought of as backwoods suavity. 'Why is it that Americans, if they're not idiots, can make us feel bumbling? Americans like Jim, for God's sake, who only got an education because there were enough hands in the cow-shed already.'

'It must be the space,' Mark said, with a note of yearning, 'and the way they move around, and talk to anybody, like Jim. You feel about someone like Jim that he's in charge of himself. So he doesn't care where he goes.'

That described so fairly the Maunoir they had just parted from that Clare wondered at his own insight into the man. It occurred to him that they must have met at a moment when Maunoir was shaken. And the reason they had met would have been that Maunoir saw in him, standing companionless, someone to ask about the green-eyed girl.

Head down, kicking at snow, he began to whistle 'La Fille aux Cheveux de Lin'. After a moment Mark joined in. They made an intricate thing of it, lifting a ringing net towards the icy branches at the head of the lane, and the small far moon and the stars like holly-leaves of light.

'Did you know,' he said, when a last chord had died for lack of breath, 'that the title is translated from Burns? "The lassie with the lint-white locks".'

'Huh,' said Mark. 'Funny you should say that.'

'Did Jim ask you about her?'

'Yes, he did. And I decided that what I told you was wrong. I don't know who she is.'

The white lane, even in the moonlight, was a gloom under its bare arching trees.

'He's made me restless,' Mark said. 'I'd like to go and be Beat, and try mescalin, and Vedanta, and be a fire-watcher in the Rockies.'

'I suppose,' Clare said, 'there's no way of combining all that with medicine.'

'I suppose not,' Mark said. 'No, I'll read about it. I'll be like bank-clerks who live on cowboy stories, and fish-and-chip-shop ladies who think a nurse's life is glamorous. Well, booy, I must now be gooin'.'

'Thanks for your company,' Clare said. 'That was a wild night for me.'

'We'll do it again,' Mark said. 'Christ, who'd have thought it could get any colder? Cheerio, dear booy – I'm orfft.'

Clare turned and plodded away down the tunnel of coralline trees. The snow, with a glaze on it, cracked and crunched under his boots, which echoed. He remembered one warm, pitch-black night of late summer when he had been sure that other footsteps were following him, and had crossed his fingers because he did not dare to turn. It infuriated Alicia, his crossing his fingers, touching wood. He told her his meaning was profound. He himself was seen by some thousands of people as a warning against the dangers of taking sorcery lightly.

Fumbling with the catch of the farm gate, he looked out over the vale. Under the sky which had cleared, and the moon which had grown so distant, the white and the black had no qualification. In that stark expanse, the lights which he had left on in the cottage asserted themselves weightily.

He made long strides down the steep field, following the path which his feet had worn through the rough pasture. At the garden gate the snow had been churned up by wistful ponies. The cottage had only one door. When it was closed behind him, he stood for a moment with his back to it. The drawbridge was up. There was nothing he loved more than the little print, from a book of voyages in the Pacific, which was there every time he returned to his castle.

In the study he crouched and shivered, reviving the grey

fire. He would need more coal for the night he saw ahead. Out
in the old brick privy, deep in evergreens, which he used for
a coal-shed, his resident wren met him with panic, like a
stranger.

When the flames were high, he climbed to his freezing
bedroom and fetched down the book. Coat and boots still on,
thawing in his decrepit armchair, he found the passage.

Tempore regis Ricardi apud Daghwurthe, in Suthfolke . . .

His eye leapt to the last words on the page.

. . . ac se Malekin vocitabat.

'Malkin,' he said aloud, gently, as if to a pet. Without
surprise, he scanned the next page for a name.

Confessa est quoque quod nata erat apud Lanaham . . .

'Ooh-ah,' he said. 'So you was born in Lavenham, gal.'

He got up and took the book to the table, and sat down on
the hard chair there. Skimming the words, he pulled paper
towards him and fumbled for a pen.

Outside, the screech owl which so often visited the oak tree
trailed a long, strangled agony across the sky. At the top of the
blank sheet he printed carefully: THE LORD ABBOT'S
TALES.

'Malkin,' he said, 'we're birds of a feather, gal. Come and
play your games with me, give me something to do.'

She spoke to him from the page. *Loquebatur autem Anglice
secundum idioma regionis illius.* He laughed aloud at her voice,
and began to write.

Concerning a
fantastic sprite

(De quodam fantastico spiritu)

In the time of King Richard, at Dagworth in Suffolk, in the house of the lord of the manor Osbern Bradwell, there appeared a fantastic sprite.

At that time the master lay in the chamber above the hall, where he had watched over the waning of the winter day, and where his death, he thought, would soon come to find him. He was a man in middle life, whose brown hair showed no grey, and whose face was made paler by the shadowing of beard which he had allowed to cloud his lean jaw. In the little light of the room his eyes were hollow, and looked before him with an expression of patience in which there was also a lessening bewilderment as he grew to feel at home with his fate.

In the hall below a log-fire leaped, and on the table one lamp cast a yellower light over the game which engaged the sick man's children. There sat the master's younger son, a child of six years, with the blue eyes of his father and with fair hair which would darken in time to his father's colour. Beside him was his sister, a girl of ten, brown-haired and brown-eyed, her child's body promising buxomness before many years. Opposite them sat their brother, the young squire, an adolescent wonderfully tall but ungainly as a foal, with the eyes of the dying man, and in his hair a ruddiness coming from his mother.

By the side of the youth sat the playfellow of his sister and brother, a girl of seven years, the motherless daughter of a neighbour. The hair of this child was fair as flax, and her eyes were of a tint between sparrow-brown and green.

The children and the young man had not been silent over their game, for there had been many treaties and parleys, and not a few hot disputes. But all that was quietness beside the difference which presently arose.

The daughter of the house spoke to her smaller brother, and said: 'You rotten cheat, Mikey; I counted then. You landed on Northumberland Avenue, and I want my rent.'

The little child, with the look of a warrior about his chin, responded: 'I did not, Lucy, and if you can't count, you can go and boil your head.'

At that the tall youth spoke, and said peaceably: 'You threw five, Mikey.'

The little fellow regarded his brother with a face swelling with rage, and cried in a great voice: 'I did *not*, Marco; I threw four.'

'Oh, let it go, Lucy,' sighed the longlegged young man. 'He knows that blackmail pays.'

'But then he'll buy Whitehall,' objected Lucy.

'I'm going to buy it,' vowed the boy.

'All right, you can,' said the youth, and took up a small card.. 'Just let's not hear any more about it.'

The child gave some brightly coloured papers to the young man, and received the card with great satisfaction. But his sister said: 'You are a baby, Mikey. Amabel's not much older than you, and she doesn't behave like that.'

'She's miles older than me,' said the boy. 'She's nearly eight.'

The little fairhaired girl placed her hand on the young man's arm, and when he had bent his head to her, whispered in his ear. He nodded at what she said, and spoke to his sister. 'Just take no notice. Otherwise – you know – he's easily upset.'

40

'Still, there *are* rules,' said the brown girl. 'Oh well, your turn, Amabel.'

The other girl threw the dice, and moved a toy thimble along the board to a place on which was written a question mark. From some cards which were piled near the centre she took the uppermost one, and privately read it, at first with puzzlement in her eyes, then with a small smile.

'It says go to gaol,' said the boy.

'No, it doesn't,' answered Amabel, and she showed it to the youth.

When he read it, the young man laughed, and seemed as puzzled as the girl. He said to himself: 'Who could have done that?' and then: 'This isn't the sort of thing you'd do, is it, Lucy?'

'What isn't?' asked the older girl, and the young man reached out a long arm and placed the card on the table between his sister and brother.

The girl stared at the card, and read aloud: 'GO AND BOIL YOUR HEAD, MIKEY.'

On hearing this, the face of the boy was vacant for a moment, then it went red and he shouted at the youth: 'Marco!'

'*I* didn't write it,' said the young man, with a convincing seriousness. 'Did you, Lucy?'

'You know I couldn't write like that. It's italic, isn't it? And I'm sure you didn't, did you, Amabel?'

The fair child shook her head, and the boy, still scowling at his brother, insisted loudly: 'I know you did, Marco, I know you did.'

Because of the passion in his voice, the brother and sister looked at one another with concern. Only the fairheaded girl, though grave and quiet, remained apart, and watched her companions with a detached curiosity.

At a moment when the youngest child seemed about to

burst into a bellow, a movement caught his eye, and he fell into stillness.

Before each of the players of the game were heaps of paper of different colours, representing money. What the child observed with round eyes was an orange paper lift itself from a pile before his brother, float across the table, and place itself on the one scrap of that colour which was his own.

Then another paper rose, from a pile before Lucy. The brown girl snatched at it in mid-air, but drew back her hand with a cry. The orange fragment continued on its way, and descended before Mikey.

Mikey began to laugh. He asked: 'What is it, how do you do it?' And from the air came an answering laugh, and a child's voice which said: '*Numquam scies.*'

The face of the brown girl, though a strong face, was full of fear, and the young man was frozen and staring. Suddenly all the play-money which lay before him and Amabel was gathered into a bundle, rose, and fell in front of Mikey. Then Lucy's money in the same way flew off, and all the wealth of the game was scattered between the hands of the boy.

Out of a box little houses of red and green wood came floating, and settled themselves with sharp clicks around the edge of the board. Then a tiny racing-car of lead, which was Mikey's counter, began to tear about the London square which had been created. It changed gear rapidly, passed each corner with screeching brakes, and at last crashed into a hotel in Mayfair. There was a hideous sound of rending metal and smashing plate-glass as the tiny car and house quite silently hit the floor.

The tall boy got to his feet, as white as a candle. He reached for the fairhaired girl's hand, and to his sister he said urgently: 'Bring Mikey, come to me.' He retreated to a high carved settle at his back, and sat stiffly down, one arm about the girl. His other arm went out to his sister, while the youngest child, between fear and laughter, made himself a redoubt of his brother's knees.

The oil-lamp on the table suddenly flared. An intense white light, in which no flame could be seen, for five seconds lit every cranny of the dark hall. Then as quickly it died, and the lamp burned peacefully on.

'Oh Marco,' Lucy whimpered. 'Oh Marco.'

One end of the great heavy settle lifted from the floor. As they slid to the other end, it sank to rest again. Then the end at which they were slumped entangled rose in its turn, to descend when their sliding had brought them to the middle.

Mikey began to scream, and Mark caught him up in his arms. Lucy would not scream, but kept moaning breathlessly.

The tall boy was sick with fear, and sick with shame at his fear. In his hoarse young mumble he cried out: 'What are you? What the hell are you?'

In the air, a child's voice called on the two notes of the cuckoo: 'Malkin.'

A door opened, and the mistress of the house came in. At the sight of her children huddled together on the settle she gave a vague smile, and asked: 'What kind of game is that?' Then she saw the face of her eldest son, and her own face stiffened and whitened. 'Marco,' she said. 'Marco – is it Daddy?'

'No,' he called out. 'No, nothing like that. It's all right. Only – '

From the table the burning lamp ascended. Its yellow light slowly circled the beamed ceiling, until it was again above the table. Then it floated down, and stood fast, without a flicker. From the air, the small voice chanted: '*Nolite timere, amiculi.*'

'Oh my God,' whispered the russet-haired lady.

But the little boy suddenly laughed, and twisting about in his brother's arms, looked expectantly into the room. Slowly, as if by no will of his, his hand lifted from his brother's, his arm stretched out, and his wrist turned. In his palm there was all at once a red apple, with a sweet smell.

'Don't eat it, Mikey,' his mother called. But the boy had already bitten into it, and chewed with content.

Unexpectedly, Amabel, who had made no sound until then, gave a tiny yelp. 'You must say thank you, Mikey,' she said. 'Thank you, thank you, whatever you are.'

Again the airy voice called, cuckoo-like: 'Malkin.'

Still white in the face, the boy in his arms, Mark stood up. He said solemnly into the air: 'In the name of the Father and of the Son and of the Holy Ghost, be gone from this house.'

Close by him there was a laugh, and the childlike voice spoke again. 'Nor don't you come to ours, you lummucken great hippeddehoy.'

'Oh, please,' cried Amabel, 'he doesn't mean to offend you.'

'I shall play with you again,' said the sprite, 'when that long lob int so fractious. I'm now going hoom.'

'But tell us who you are,' cried the fairhaired girl.

From the open door behind the lady there came again the cuckoo-call of: 'Malkin.' It was repeated several times before dying away in distant rooms.

The young man and his mother looked large-eyed at one another. In the mistress's face was a dwindling fear, which was letting in amusement. In the youth's, fear was vanquished by mortification.

'I *felt* it,' Lucy exclaimed, suddenly garrulous with relief. 'I grabbed at the money it had in its hand, and it snatched it away, but I'd felt its fingers. Tiny fingers.'

Amabel said shyly: 'It pulled at – it snapped my knicker-elastic. Then it whispered in my ear: "Lot of thanks I get." It meant from Mikey.'

The little boy was still skranshing the spirit's apple.

'Mikey,' his mother said, 'what did it say to you?'

'It was like this,' the child said, and putting his lips against his brother's ear blew a raspberry. 'That's what made me laugh,' he explained. 'It sounded like that, and I could feel this nice warm mouth.'

In the chamber above the hall the sick man lay in the uncurtained four-poster bed. His melancholy eyes, in a face made the finer by his wraith of a beard, were on the sunny window, and on the tall black figure which stood looking over the walled garden.

'It will soon be spring,' said the man in black clothes. 'I see some daffodils out around your fruit trees.'

'So early?' said the man in the bed. 'How sudden everything seems to be this year.'

The priest, turning back from the outlook, strayed to a chair placed by the bed, and lowered on to it his large, athletic frame. He was a man perhaps ten years younger than the other, with a strong face in which there was nevertheless something ingenuous. The eyes of the older man rested on him for a moment with an ambiguous expression, mingling indulgence with respect.

'Do you have anything you want to say to me?' the priest asked. 'Any question?'

The gaunt man shook his head with a smile in which there was still something boyish. 'Why disturb our peace of mind?'

'My peace is nothing,' said the big priest. 'But if that's a consideration with you, you could think about making me feel useful.'

'Ah, no,' said the master of the house. 'I couldn't think about that. Because it's calm here, where I am. You're the stronger man. At a time like this, don't disturb me by asking for my help.'

The big man seemed made graver, and uncertain, by his friend, but after a moment smiled at him fraternally, and said: 'You don't change. No. Ornery as mud.'

In the hall below Amabel and Mikey sat at the table, while their mother's daily aide whisked about them with duster and broom. 'I don't know, I'm sure,' she said, 'why you sit here just when I'm busy. It's a lovely morning out, if you wrap up well.'

'We're waiting, Mrs Kersey,' said Mikey. 'We've been waiting since breakfast.'

'For a friend,' explained Amabel, 'who is coming to play.'

'Well, the play-room is tidy,' said Mrs Kersey, 'and I'm sure that's easier to keep warm. That fire make so much dust in here.'

As the rosy woman, with duster and furniture-polish, was addressing herself to the oak settle, a voice said out of the air: 'Did you ever find your ring, Kitty Kersey?'

Mikey ran to the door, yelling: 'Lucy! Lucy!' And Mrs Kersey suddenly found Amabel beside her, holding her protectively by the hand.

With the smile of someone whose good humour was being tested in public, Mrs Kersey gazed about the ceiling. 'Am I on Candid Camera?' she asked. 'Well, if that's you, Mark, I've heard of tape-recorders before.'

'It int Mark,' said the voice from the air. 'You don't know me, but I know you, Kitty Kersey.'

'It's that familiar,' said Mrs Kersey. 'If it's you, Lucy, I shall give you a good slap.'

'It int Lucy, neither,' said the voice. 'Lucy's just now coming.' And a moment later the brown girl arrived in haste.

'Is it Malkin?' she panted out to Amabel, and the other girl nodded her pale gold head.

Mrs Kersey's tolerant face was beginning to look imposed upon, and she said a little fretfully: 'If it's a joke, there's jokes that go off, like milk.'

'Now then, Kitty Kersey,' said the sprite, 'don't get your knickers in a twist. There int so many people see as are sin, and I believe I've sin you about for a year or two. Not to mention the times I've heard your name from Bill Brooks up at the forge. Old Bill he say: "If ever I marry again," he say, "Kitty

46

Bugg that was will be the bride, and no other won't do." '

'The cheek of him,' bridled Mrs Kersey. 'He's got no right to be making so free with my name, and he can't say that I ever give him encouragement.'

'I don't say you do, gal,' answered Malkin, 'and he don't say so, and he only talk like that to his old mother, and she's as deaf as a beetle. But old Bill, he int such a bad old boy, and he fancies you something comical, and widowers int so thick on the ground as widows. There's others would have him, and Margery Mill is one.'

'She's very welcome, I'm sure,' said Mrs Kersey.

'I'll tell you something,' said Malkin, 'I hear about Margery Mill. Cor, I thought I'd die laughing. It was during the war, you see, when the Yanks was about with lots of money, and that Margery Clegg, she was then, she give herself a bath in milk. A bathful of milk, I ask you, would you credit it? Iss, she bathed in milk to make herself more beautiful.'

'She never!' cried Mrs Kersey, with joyous laughter. 'Oh, I don't believe it. How could you know such a thing?'

'I was in her sister's house,' said Malkin, 'when she tell her husband that story, and I had to go away because I thought they'd hear me laughing. There int many I talk to,' explained the sprite, 'and none that see me. But a house like this, with children in it, is kind of cheery, and it's dismal-like at ours.'

'Malkin,' said Lucy, 'where do you live?'

'Here and there, dear gal,' said the sprite, 'here and there. I've been at Kitty Kersey's before now, when her daughter was younger. I sin Kitty lose her ring, and I know where it is.'

'My ring?' cried Mrs Kersey.

'Iss,' answered Malkin, 'that cheap little old ring your Tom give you when you was walking out. That roll under your bed and down a crack, and if your son-in-law lift a board, there it will be.'

While Mrs Kersey exclaimed her thanks, Amabel was

watching the stairs. The tall priest was descending, with a thoughtful face, and fingering his lip.

'Morning, Mrs K.,' he said absently; and then, puzzled by the scene in the hall: 'Was it me you were speaking to then?'

'Oh, it's just some game,' said Mrs Kersey, ill at ease. 'No, I didn't even see you there.'

Malkin said distinctly: '*Abes, praelonge!*'

'Excuse me?' said the priest, looking amazed. 'What was that?'

Again the high, childlike voice cried out commandingly: '*Abes, praelonge!*'

'I see,' said the priest, looking, however, quite baffled. 'Mark has taught one of you to say – er – "Make off, Lofty!" in Latin.'

'*Mentiris,*' said Malkin irritably. '*Marcus haud Latine loqui potest.*'

'It's got to be Mark,' said the priest, more and more uncomfortable. 'How are you doing that voice, Mark? Where are you hiding?'

'*Attende,*' said Malkin, with authority. '*Aliquid tecum volo disceptare.*'

Suddenly the large man drifted across the room, his soles an inch from the floor, and disposed himself upon the settle. He sat blank-faced and with twitching fingers while the sprite poured over him a stream of Latin.

'*Satis!*' he protested at last, raising a hand in surrender. '*Vicisti. Amplius non possum.*'

'It do go on,' said Mrs Kersey sympathetically. 'But why don't you speak English to the gentleman? It can,' she explained. 'It's proper Suffolk.'

'Tell us what it said, Father Jacques,' Lucy called out. 'Tell us what Malkin said.'

'Malkin?' he repeated. 'Is that what you call it: Malkin?'

From high in the ceiling, the width of the room away, came the cuckoo-call.

48

'Malkin,' said Mrs Kersey. 'A real old country word that is. My granny used to call a scarecrow a mawkin.'

'I int no scarecrow, gal,' said the sprite. 'I'm a bouncing baby.'

'A baby!' the priest exclaimed; while Lucy asked, tenderly: 'Are you a boy or a girl?'

'Did you ever hear,' demanded the testy spirit, 'of a boy called Malkin, you noddy?'

'But Malkin,' said the priest, looking up at the ceiling with troubled eyes, 'Malkin, you just preached me a sermon in Latin on the doctrine of original sin, and on the possibility of the redemption of Satan at the Last Day, and you supported your argument in favour of that hypothesis with considerable learning, as far as I could follow.'

'We int all Swedes in Suffolk,' said the spirit-child.

'Malkin, how old are you?' asked Mikey, his favourite question.

'Thass a bit hard to say, dear boy,' replied the sprite. 'But if you all will listen to me right quiet, I shall tell you how I come here.

'I was born,' she said, 'in Lavenham, and my mam was miserable poor. One day she took me to the beet-field, where she was hoeing weeds for the farmer, as I expect you've sin the gypsy women doing, young Mikey. I was one year old, and I never give her much trouble. So she put me down to sleep under an ash tree at the edge of the field, and she and the other women got on with the work.

'Well, I don't remember a lot, but I woke up and I was crying. An ant had bit me or summut like that, and I skreeked. I bellowed like I've heard you do, you young foghorn. And all of a sudden this woman come, and she grab me.

'I was wholly surprised, because this old gal warnt nothing like my mam. And I held my noise, I was that frightened I had to.

49

'Well, this old gal she take me hoom with her, and I live there still. I won't tell you where, but that int so very far from here. The old gal she don't treat me too bad, and I've had some jokes with her son, the young layabout, and I call them my mother and brother, though they int.

'But one thing that make them awkward, thass me going out to the houses of human beings. That get right up their noses, that do, they being differently made. Oh, I shall be jawed tonight when I go hoom, and I hope he don't take his belt to me. The old gal, you see, she's a witch, and so is he.'

The spirit paused, and after a moment Lucy asked gently: 'Are you always invisible, Malkin?'

'No, gal, I int,' said the sprite. 'But I steal their cap, and thass what it mainly is that get their rags out. They have this cap, you see, that make you invisible. Many's the hiding I had, Kitty Kersey, for the time I spent with your daughter.'

'And how long,' asked Lucy, 'have you lived in their house?'

'Seven year,' said Malkin, and her bright voice grew drab with sadness. 'I thought when the seventh year was up I should go hoom. But all my hopes was dashed, as the saying goes. So here I am waiting for seven more years from now. Or it might be seven from then, or seven from that, or never.'

'Oh Malkin, Malkin,' said Lucy, with misty eyes.

'Cheer up, my treasure,' said Malkin; 'it int so bad being a witch. But I'm still very young, and my heart's with mankind, somehow. I should like to live among them, and be one myself. *Ad pristinam hominum cohabitationem,*' she elaborated to the priest, *'volo reverti.'*

'My child,' said the priest, in halting and canine Latin, 'are you a Christian?'

'I believe I am,' she replied in the same tongue. 'Why do you ask?'

'There is a man upstairs whom you might console.'

'When the time is ripe,' said the spirit-child, 'and he will

50

welcome me. Then I will go with him hand in hand, to the gate.'

'God bless you, Malkin,' said the big man, in English. 'I'd like to kiss you for that.'

'Malkin,' said Lucy, 'Malkin, may *I* kiss you?'

'Not yet, gal, not yet,' said the invisible child in a whisper. When her voice came again it was far away in the air. 'What kind of thanks is that, to make Malkin cry?'

With the weeks that passed, as the garden beneath the sick man's windows swelled into spring, the company of Malkin became such a habit with the household that its mistress would say, not looking up from her recipe-book: 'Be an angel, Malkin, go and pinch me some tarragon from Lady Munby's.' Or Mrs Kersey would say: 'Malkin, take this duster, gal, and do the picture rails.' For such tasks the sprite received her meals, which were always placed on the settle in the hall, and which simply disappeared, though half a dozen pairs of eyes watched like kestrels.

She would come upon them also far from the house. One black night Mark was walking down Hole Lane to visit a friend at the farm, picking his way with tentative feet through dark so intense that he could distinguish nothing. Suddenly it seemed to him that the echoes of his footsteps between the budding trees had themselves an echo, that he was followed. From the thought of that person or fiend, his mind turned in a moment to Old Shuck, the fiend-dog. Presently he was certain that he could hear slavering snorts from its muzzle, below the flaming eyes.

Then a high clear voice that he knew began to sing.

> 'Still, be thou still,
> Poorest of all, stern one;
> Nor shalt thou, Old Shuck,
> Moot with me no more.

51

'But fly, sorrowful thing,
Out of mine eynesight,
And dive thither where thou
Man may domáge no more.'

'Malkin, you bitch,' the long youth said. 'Then it was you I heard making Shuck noises behind me.'

'Only little ones,' said the sprite. 'I just wanted to terrify you a bit.'

'That was friendly,' said the young man. 'What a queer old charm you sang then. As if you were sad for the shuck-dog.'

'So I am, boy,' said the invisible child. 'Thass a poor old miserable thing, the shuck-dog. That roam over Suffolk and Norfolk with its eyes on fire and its mouth dripping, big as a calf, scaring people to death. And thass ever so unhappy.'

'Malkin, do you know Old Shuck?'

'Of course I know him,' Malkin said impatiently. 'And right sorrowful he is without his master. Never got over the death of his master, Old Shuck didn't. His master was the god Odin over in Denmark. Know Old Shuck? I should just think I did. And the Nun of Bures, and the Hairy Presence, and the Knights Templar of Coggeshall, and I don't know how many more.'

'Malkin,' said Mark, 'do demons and ghosts – and sprites – necessarily tell the truth?'

'No, mate, we don't,' said the sprite. 'But I'm telling you history, if you'd wash out your brains and listen.'

The young man walked on, until the trees were behind him, and the farm, dim but distinct, spread out below. 'Good night, Malkin,' he said, though he sensed that she was gone. When he arrived at the cottage, his friend stared at the daisy-chain with which Malkin had crowned his hair.

The narrow timbered house in a Lavenham street was leaning at all sorts of impossible angles, but looked sound and lovingly cared for. Knocking at the heavy door, the priest noticed clean white curtains beside him, and between them a proudly blooming hyacinth.

At his second knock the door opened. He thought at first that he had made a mistake, and asked uncertainly: 'Mrs Burrows?'

'Yes,' said the young woman. She was not more than twenty-one, neat in her dress, her black hair carefully arranged.

'I'm sorry,' the priest said, 'to turn up like this on your doorstep without warning. But I'd be grateful if you would spare me a few minutes to discuss something, out of the street.'

'I'm not – ' the young woman began to say. But reflecting, she stepped back and led him into the tiny hall which had been contrived in the old cottage. From there she led the way into her front room, which the priest found solidly furnished, not quite according to his own taste, but showing a modest prosperity.

He took the chair she offered, and said: 'This visit must be something of a surprise.'

The woman sat down opposite him, not curious, her face rather bland. 'I should think it would be on account of some girl,' she said, 'and one of my brothers.'

'There is a girl involved,' said the priest. 'A very young girl. Mrs Burrows, I learn from my inquiries that seven years ago you became the mother of a daughter called Mary, or Malkin.'

The woman immediately became sullen, which brought out a childishness in her face. 'I don't see how that come to be a concern of yours.'

'You were extremely young,' suggested the priest.

'I was fourteen,' said Mrs Burrows. 'Are you going to ask if I was married?'

'No, Mrs Burrows, I know the answer to that. I also know that the child mysteriously vanished.'

'No one can't blame that on me,' the young woman said, a

shrillness in her voice. 'I know there's plenty would like to believe I dropped her in a pond or something. But I was in the middle of a field with three other women when that happen. They all live here, they all will vouch for me.'

'I know,' said the priest, 'that in such cases the mother's distress is often made all the more cruel by gossip, suspicion. Unfortunately, on some occasions the suspicion has been justified. But I believe, Mrs Burrows – I *know* – that no blame of that kind attaches to you. The baby was sleeping under a tree at the edge of the field you mention. Did you see anybody go near it?'

'No,' said the woman, firmly. 'There warnt nobody there but us four women, all working together.'

The priest opened out on his black knees a book which he had been carrying, and ran an eye over the neat lines of his handwriting.

'Mrs Burrows,' he said, 'I'd like to tell you, in my own words, another mother's story.'

'If that's short,' the woman said indifferently. 'My husband come home at noon.'

'This story is from a source we consider reliable,' said the priest. 'The reporter is Roger of Howden. It concerns a young unmarried mother-to-be who ran away from her parents' house just as her condition was about to reveal itself.'

'Your story int all that uncommon,' remarked Mrs Burrows.

'On the road,' continued the priest, 'she was overtaken by a violent storm of wind and rain. And as she was wandering lost among the fields, she cried out to God to give her help and shelter. But when God did not instantly answer, she prayed instead: "If God will not hear my prayers, *let the Devil succour me.*"'

'Oh-ah,' said Mrs Burrows calmly. 'Well, a girl in such a fix wouldn't be all that choosey.'

'Immediately there appeared to her a youth with bare feet,

girded up for the road, and he said to her: "Follow me." That prepossessing youth, Mrs Burrows, was the Devil.'

'You make him sound quite nice,' observed Mrs Burrows.

'In the fields they found a sheepfold, and the Devil went ahead of the girl and made a fire and prepared her a couch of fresh straw; and when the girl had come in and warmed herself, she said: "I'm tormented by hunger and thirst." The Devil said: "Wait a little, and I will bring you food and drink." But while he was away, three wayfarers who had been surprised by the firelight came into the sheepfold, and asked the gravid woman who had made the fire. She replied: "The Devil." When they asked her where he was, she answered: "I was hungry and thirsty, and he went to find me food and drink."

'At this the three travellers exclaimed: "Have faith in Our Lord Jesus Christ, and in the glorious Virgin Mary His mother, and they will deliver you out of the hands of the enemy." And they then went away to a village which was nearby, and told what they had heard and seen to the clerk and people.

'In the meantime the Devil returned, and comforted the woman with bread and water, and when her body was arched in labour, the Devil, acting as midwife, received her son, and warmed him at the fire.

'But the priest of the village I have mentioned, armed with the catholic faith and the Cross and the holy water, came with the clerk and many of the people to the sheepfold, and found the woman just delivered of a boy-child, which the Devil was holding in his arms. At once the priest sprinkled the holy water, in the name of the Holy Trinity and each of its Persons. And from this the Devil, being unable to endure it, fled, *carrying the boy with him*, and was seen by them no more. And the woman, coming to her senses, said: "Now I know the truth, because the Lord has snatched me out of the hand of the enemy."'

'Well, you need say no more,' said Mrs Burrows, with a

grim mouth. 'I shall answer the question you come here to ask. Yes, I did have Malkin baptized, though it went against the grain, knowing that "baseborn", or worse, might be written in the register. Do that contribute to ease your curiosity?'

'It does, very considerably,' replied the priest. 'But if you'll bear with me just a little longer, I'd like to tell you of another case, reported by someone well known to us, Gervase of Tilbury.

'This case took place in Catalonia, in the diocese of Gerona, at a village called La Junquera. In that region there is a high and difficult mountain, its summit containing a lake whose bottom cannot be seen through the almost black water. This is said to be the gate to a dwelling-place of demons, and if a stone is dropped into the water there is immediately a storm, as if the demons were enraged. On one part of the peak there is perpetual snow and ice, for the sun never reaches there. At the foot of the mountain is a river, whose sands contain gold, which the local people call *palleol*.

'Lately, reports Gervase, an agricultural worker called Pedro Cabina, who was attending to domestic matters in his house, was driven to distraction by the continual and implacable howling of his little daughter, and exclaimed: "May the demons fly off with her!" This ejaculation was heard, and immediately a crowd of invisible demons made off with the child.'

Mrs Burrows' face was stricken. Her eyes, avoiding the priest, tried to find comfort in her carefully tended hyacinth, while her fingers played with a fold of her dress.

'Seven years from that time,' continued the priest, 'a neighbour of Pedro Cabina's met, near the sinister mountain, a man who was running along, crying in a lamentable voice: "Woe's me, ah wretched me, how have I deserved to be crushed with such a load?" Pedro's neighbour asked the cause of his distress, and he answered that for seven years he had lived in that mountain, at the disposal of demons, who used him every day as a beast of burden. When the other showed incredulity, he added that in the same mountain the demons held in servile bondage a girl, the daughter of Pedro Cabina of La Junquera. But the demons were tired of training her, and would freely restore her to her curser, if the father would reclaim her from the mountain.

'Though still incredulous, the neighbour sought out Pedro at La Junquera, and found him even then lamenting the long absence of his daughter. When the reason for her absence was explained, the neighbour told the father what he knew, and suggested that Pedro, under the protection of the Divine Name, seek his vanished daughter in the mountain.

'Pedro, though amazed, decided to take his advice. Having climbed the mountain and reached the lake, he sought out the demons, and begged that they restore the girl. Thereupon, as if carried by a sudden blast, his daughter came forth: long of stature, dried-up, noisome, with wandering eyes, with bones and nerves and skin scarcely hanging together, horrid in aspect, speech and intellect, and knowing and understanding hardly anything human.

'Having received her, the bewildered father sought the counsel of the bishop of Gerona; and that good man exhibited her before his flock, exhorting them never to commend anyone to the demons. For the Devil our adversary, as a roaring lion seeking whom he may devour, destroys some, namely those given to him, whom he then holds imprisoned without hope of redemption; while others, such as those cursed, he merely torments and afflicts for a time.

'I will not, Mrs Burrows,' continued the priest, 'detain you with what exactly was seen in the dwelling-place of the demons by the man they used as a beast of burden: an intelligent man, later released through the agency of Pedro Cabina. Suffice it to say that those who are casually sent to the Devil by others may find themselves, if the wrong ears hear, in a sense *half* damned, though kept apart from those devoted to eternal perdition. And sadly, those *commendati*, as we call them, are usually children. I have cases here from Sweden, from Serbia, from Germany. A happier story, the German one. Though both parents cursed the child, the Devil, who happened to be there, remarked: "They wouldn't take two thousand pounds for it, really." There are numerous such cases in Russia, of which Tooke writes: "The beings so stolen are neither fiends nor men; they are invisible, and afraid of the Cross and holy water; but on the other hand, in their nature and disposition they resemble mankind, whom they love, and rarely injure."'

The priest paused; but seeing that the young woman kept her eyes stubbornly on the window, he resumed: 'A moment of temper is not blamed by anybody, Mrs Burrows. But from the story of Pedro Cabina's daughter, and from something said by Malkin herself, I believe that you might have reclaimed her recently, and that she expected it.'

'Oh-ah,' said the woman. 'Something said by Malkin. Sin her, have you?'

'Not seen, Mrs Burrows. Malkin is invisible to us. But I have spoken with her. She is a naturally happy child who will not show her misery. But I feel her homesickness, and I know that she hopes in seven years' time, fourteen years after your unfortunate expression, to come home to you.'

The woman rose, and going to the window ledge made some small adjustment to the position of the pink flowers. Looking out into the street, she said: 'She won't never come here. Never.'

'I see,' said the priest.

'What I said that day,' said the woman, 'I meant. There was I, a mother of fifteen, working my guts out for a brat I never wanted, without decent clothes to my back, without even much hope of a husband. When she started yelling, I say to myself, quite loud: "Mischief take the squawling bastard." You ask if I sin anything. Well, I did. I sin that little bundle lift off the ground and disappear, and my heart was as light as a feather. I got my husband in the end, I got my house and my clothes, and I shall keep them. My husband know there was a child, but there int one now and there int no trouble between us. If she come, but she won't, I should bolt the door against her.'

The priest carefully closed his book, and sat drumming with his fingers on its cover. 'But after all, Mrs Burrows, flesh and blood — '

The young woman laughed harshly. 'There int no happy memories for me in that flesh and blood. She come of a rape, and by someone I hate like you hate the Devil.'

'I see,' said the priest again. 'Perhaps someone related to you?'

'Like you say, you see,' said the woman.

The priest got up, and stood uneasy in the room, whose low beams oppressed him. 'Then I must take up no more of your time.'

'Let me show you to the door,' said Malkin's mother, going past him.

On the step, in the breezy cold sunlight of the street, the priest said: 'There is a point on which you may feel easy, Mrs Burrows. I can't admire your later conduct, but by having Malkin baptized you have probably saved her from being lost eternally.'

'I should have undone that,' said the woman, 'if I could. There it stay now, in black and white, for any nosey vicar or clerk to look at. I shall kick myself for that one day, I know. But you see, I warnt so sharp at fourteen as I hope I am now.'

The priest watched as the heavy door closed, with a clash of oak and iron.

For weeks there had been between Malkin and Lucy something from which the others, aware of silences falling suddenly when they entered rooms in which the two were, felt excluded. For the brown girl, who still cherished her dolls, was of a motherly mould, and something in the spirit-child, things which were never said, had touched her as she had not been touched before by anything but her pony. So whispered confabulations took place, and gifts were exchanged, of choice spring flowers and special titbits of food, such as Lucy's homemade toffee, and the facetious sprite was at home with the rather solemn girl as she was with no one else.

There came a morning, as Lucy on her pony ambled down a ride through Lady Munby's woods, where the spirit spoke to her from a budding chestnut. Her voice was a little sad, as though with resignation. She said: 'Lucy, I have been thinking of what you want, and you shall have it. When you are in your bed tonight, I shall come.'

As soberly, the girl said: 'Thank you, Malkin,' and rode on in silence under the trees swelling with promise.

But the matter occupied her thoughts all day, and she went early to bed, and waited with a grave expectation, a small nightlight faintly infiltrating the shadows of her room.

When the sprite came, her voice seemed to rise almost from the floor, as if a very small child stood by the bed. She said: 'You won't touch me, Lucy? You won't grab me, promise?'

'No, Malkin,' said the girl, 'I've promised you already.'

'Will you swear it, gal, by the Holy Trinity and all the persons of it?'

'I swear,' Lucy said, 'by the Father, Son and Holy Ghost.'

'Then look where my voice come from,' said the spirit, 'and you shall see.'

Beside the bed a luminosity began to shape itself. Its outlines cleared, and Malkin was within reach of Lucy's hand.

She was in form a child of twelve months old, dressed in a white frock, smiling uncertainly but with a beseeching sweetness at the girl who leaned from her bed towards her. Her hair was fine and black, her eyes so light in colour that they seemed silver. With a timid movement she raised one miniature hand, as if to ward off the girl's advance. On the wrist was a bracelet, of gold discs half as big as a farthing, each with a hieroglyph or symbol engraved upon it.

'Remember,' she said, 'you swore.'

But the girl would not be stopped. 'Oh you poor, pretty baby,' she said, 'how can it hurt if I give you a kiss?' Her arm curved about the small figure and touched it, ready to draw it towards her.

'No!' cried Malkin; and suddenly she was no longer there.

'Malkin!' the girl called out. 'Oh don't — don't be angry. I was silly, I was wicked. But I won't again, I won't break my word again.' Slipping from her bed, standing on the mat, she watched all the space of the room for a sign.

'Hush,' said the spirit from the air, with all her old childish authority. 'Hush now, I'm listening.'

A low, soothing croon floated down from the shadows. The door, which was slightly ajar, stirred on its hinges. Lucy, padding after the sound, followed the dark passage, cold under her bare feet, until she had reached her father's door.

The door was closed. The crooning had died away. Suddenly, through the oak, the girl heard the call of a cuckoo. She listened smiling, thinking that she knew what had made it. But it came again, and then she recognized the voice of a real cuckoo, somewhere out beyond her father's window, in the garden's nightbound trees.

APRIL

The cuckoo had for Clare of all touches the most magicianly, the most transforming. When he lay in his bed in the early mornings, looking out from his pillow over the clearing of the old fishponds, the cuckoo with its frail assertiveness expanded everything, till the wood grew huge as the ancient man-scaring forest of High Suffolk, and the sound was a tender green.

At the edge of each window the apple tree, agitated by bullfinches, intruded branches of tight flushed buds. In the nearest field the combed bay earth was lined with the first spears of barley, and the poplars on the horizon had about them now a copper-coloured mist.

He thought on one such morning, listening to the cuckoo, that his provisional happiness had put down roots, that the fact of it would endure.

The unfamiliar sound of the telephone drove the cuckoo out of his head. Wrong number he thought, or Mikey; and made his way downstairs in no hurry, since Mikey would hang on for ever.

'Clare,' he said, and waited for Mikey Clare to say: 'Snap.'

'Clare?' a man's voice verified. 'Good morning, Clare. This is somebody from your past.'

'Oh?' Clare said. 'I don't appear to remember you.'

'Perry,' said the voice.

'Perry?' Clare said doubtfully. 'Perry who? Wait a moment. Do you mean Matthew Perry?'

'Yes, that one,' the man said. 'So the old school hasn't been blotted out of your mind entirely.'

'I wasn't there long enough,' Clare said, 'to be marked too indelibly. But who wouldn't remember you, Matt?'

'I want to see you,' Perry said. 'Is that a possibility?'

'Of course it is. Where are you —London? Can you come here?'

'That's what I'd planned,' Perry said. 'On Saturday morning, I thought. Could you put me up for a night?'

'Not too luxuriously, but I can borrow a bed. It's kind of rough here, I warn you. I can't cook, and live as if I was still in the bush. I don't know what you're used to. What do you do these days?'

'I'm a financier's punk,' Perry said, 'or righthand man, as he has it. We're in minerals, oil and such stuff. Don't worry, I know something about living in the bush, on several continents. Suppose I take the 10.30 from Liverpool Street, could you meet me at the station?'

'Yes, of course. On foot, probably. It's a three-mile walk across the fields, if you're up to it. But how did you find me?'

'We have our methods,' Perry said. 'Actually, I rang the only C. Clare in the book, and spoke to two children called Mikey and Lucy. Very sensible girl, Lucy. She says you're much better, whatever she meant by that.'

'Yes, I am,' Clare said. 'So you must know any news I have.'

'Not from you,' Perry said. 'You'll be at the station, then, on Saturday? I think I remember that station. Stuck out in the fields, with no reason you can see for being there.'

'That's the one,' Clare said, and hung fire, wondering how to keep up a conversation with a man he had not seen since their teens. 'Well, Matt.'

'Well, Clare,' Perry said, 'I won't hold you up. But what is it like where you are?'

'Through the window, from where I'm standing,' Clare said, 'I can see a mass of lilacs, not in flower yet. On the lawn,

66

as you might call it, there's an infant rabbit nibbling. There's also, usually, a magnificent cock-pheasant strutting about, and a stoat of a very tender age which seems to want someone to play with it. The birds never let up from first light, but what seems to fill the house is the noise of wood-pigeons. If I held the receiver away you could probably hear them. "Over his own sweet voice the Stock-dove broods" — remember?'

'Oh God, yes. Old Pickers and his country pieties. He'd be proud of you. Well, Clare, I did say I wouldn't keep you.'

'On Saturday, then,' Clare said. 'Matt — I'm very glad you rang.'

'So am I,' said Perry. 'It's been aeons, C.C. In case you've forgotten me, I'll be wearing the *Financial Times*. Till then.'

Putting down the receiver, Clare stood watching the little rabbit in the new grass and the weeds. A jay, with a flash of blue from its wing, swooped threatening near, and the bundle of fur threw itself up in fright, then vanished into the lilac hedge.

When he had washed and breakfasted, Clare went out into the pigeon-moaning garden. In its rough meadow-grass daffodils were beginning to fade, and a few tulips were fiercely agape. The one part of it which he tended was crammed with wallflowers, and their scent came almost violently to his reformed smoker's nose.

A tractor came racketing down the hill on the road leading to the farmhouse, and John waved and bawled: 'How do.' The farm's Alsatian was loping beside, but with a change of interest made off to see Clare, leaping the gate which was closed against ponies. Clare bent to pat the hard body squirming against his legs, and said as his face was flannelled with a tongue: 'Dead soppy, aren't you?'

With the big dog prancing ahead, he crossed the stream and took the farm track towards the marsh, between the green-misted wood and a hedgerow frosted with blackthorn flowers. At the edge of the wood, leaning out over the green road, a tall wild cherry caught the breath with its drifts of white bloom. He stood and stared up at it, the sight of its smooth limbs like a tactile pleasure, while now and again a papery flower fluttered down.

There was a crash in the hedgerow, and turning, he saw among primroses the Alsatian's rear-end, violently absorbed. Then the dog bounded back, and he caught a glimpse of crimson, a flash of metallic viridian from the neck-feathers of the pheasant. Before he could think, the bird was crunched down, bolted, gone. Only a wing remained, hanging hideously from the dog's jaws.

'Oh, you horror,' he groaned. 'Oh, you shuck-dog, you.'

He was afraid that the dog would choke, and moved to help her. But she gulped a few times, and the wing with its coarse feathers disappeared. She stood for a while with an air of thoughtfulness, then ambled off preoccupied towards her home.

Clare walked on to the marsh, where the dank green was yellow-starred with celandine, white-starred with stitchwort, and where catkins hung from the willows. It had been his own cock-pheasant, he felt sure, the constant visitor which had marched so masterfully under his windows. What at one time would have sickened him he could now once more take with calm. It was the way of the green god.

That evening he walked with Alicia through the dusk for an early drink at the Shoulder of Mutton. As they took the path through the churchyard he noticed a woman standing among the headstones, and even in the dim light recognized her by the ghostly fairness of her hair.

In a low voice he asked Alicia: 'Do you see that girl? Do you know who she is?'

Alicia glanced as they passed her, but said: 'No, I don't. Of course, her back was turned, but her figure wasn't at all familiar. I should have remembered that hair.'

'Mark thought she was an au pair at Lady Munby's.'

'I'm sure she's not. I noticed the current au pair because she's Swedish and she's dark, which surprised me. But she might be the au pair's chum. And then, other people besides Lady Munby have them.'

'She made a definite impression,' Clare said, as they passed out at the other gate, 'on Jim-Jacques.'

'Oh, Jim-Jacques,' said Alicia enthusiastically. 'That dishy man. Lucy was besotted with him. We missed him sorely for a while. Do you hear from him?'

'Yes,' Clare said, 'he's written once. He's living in a shack in the woods in Maine. Everything's still under snow there, and he gets about on skis. He hasn't a car. We've met a prodigy: a penniless American.'

'I wish he'd come back,' Alicia said. 'Lucy, and Mikey too, found him very comforting. Tell him that.'

'He'd like to know,' said Clare; and they strolled on towards the pub's welcoming windows, which stared Old Shuck-like through the twilight, hellfire-red.

On the station's breezy platform, with a wide view over the fields, Clare ran into John. 'Hullo,' he said, 'have you taken to travelling?'

'I suppose this is how you dress when you go up to Lunnon,' said John. He was wearing muddy blue overalls tucked into his Wellingtons, and his hair, which always looked as if it should have straw in it, did have some. 'I'm meeting my sister,' he explained. 'You know, Mildred, she work in the Post Office.'

'Is she your sister?' Clare said. 'It would take me years to sort out the Swainstead families.'

The signals changed, and the train rattled in, to halt at the opposite platform. Doors slammed, but nobody could be seen until the whistle sounded and the train was off again. Then a handful of people began to cross the walkway over the lines, and among them Clare recognized Mildred, with two small children at her skirts. Behind her walked a man in a leather jacket and cavalry twill trousers, carrying an incongruous and expensive briefcase.

Clare went down the platform, giving Mildred a greeting as he passed, towards the man in the leather jacket. The man's face had a respectable gravity, it was a face designed for strangers. All at once it was split by a crazy white grin.

'Clare,' Perry said, and crushed the hand which was offered to him. Clare remembered the bleak grey of his eyes, and how suddenly they could come alight.

There were people who thought Matthew Perry a handsome young man. With the adolescent Perry Clare's own mother had been somewhat smitten. To Clare himself it had always seemed that there was something faintly simian about his friend, about the long-armed athletic body and the almost too expressive features. Matthew Perry was a nutter, his contemporaries said, sensing in him uncomfortable reserves of emotion. But to his elders, paradoxically, it had always been his control which impressed, his relentless working towards any object he had chosen.

'Well,' he said, 'here we are, old Clare.'

'Yes, here we are,' said Clare, inanely, and wondered what else to say. Nothing had changed, only faces had firmed, perhaps hardened.

'Cris,' John called out, 'do you want a ride hoom, boy? The gaffer lend me the Landrover today.'

'No, thanks, John,' Clare called back. 'We're going to get some exercise.'

Perry's gaze was sharp and amused, watching John and Mildred depart. 'I say,' he said, 'I fancy that blue-eyed ploughboy.'

'What do you mean?' asked Clare, puzzled, and then realized. 'Oh Jesus. I thought you'd have grown out of that.'

'I cause no scandal,' Perry promised him. 'Come on, let's go "hoom", as he calls it.'

Out of the shadow of the station the sun was palely bright. The yards and the embankment were tangled with flowering periwinkles, an elusive blue fleeting into mauve. They walked by a line of poplars, whose translucent new leaves overhead glowed auburn. Across a field of young beans were the outbuildings of a substantial farm, and the patterned brickwork of their walls stirred a memory in Clare, until he remembered his

70

prep-school days in Western Australia, where the early settlers had seemed to have a passion for such games with bricks, which he thought he had heard called diapering.

They climbed a stile and took a footpath skirting raw cornfields, beside hedgerows white with blackthorn and may. Then they were out in a marshy field, being stared at by lumpish Friesian cattle, some of which strayed after them to the earth dike bounding the river. There a breeze, smelling of the sea, bent the rushes, and as they crossed a short bridge a great cob-swan hissed at them haughtily.

Plodding up a hill, growing short-winded, Perry said: 'Someone spread a rumour that Suffolk was flat.'

'That int,' Clare said. 'I ride a pushbike, so I know.'

At another stile, near the top of the rise, he paused and said: 'Take a breather, Matt.' From where they stood a footpath ran diagonally down a new barley field to the level of the valley again. 'You can't see the farm yet,' he said, pointing, 'but it's around the corner of that wood.'

The trees below would later darken and have, in the humid summer air, a tinge of blue, almost black. But now all was softest green and silver, except where, far off, there flared the chrome yellow of a mustard field. Between willows, the distant river meandered towards the next village, whose high church tower was flying a huge flag, a vermilion cross on white. 'St George's Day,' Clare realized. 'Happy birthday, Shakespeare.'

Perry pulled out cigarettes, then slapped his sides. 'Got a light, C.C.?'

Clare felt in the pocket of his donkey-jacket, then remembered that he did not smoke. 'Sorry,' he said. But Perry had found what he wanted, a gold Dunhill lighter, and leaned on the stile ebbing blue clouds.

Clare stared at what he had found in his pocket. Of course, a pack of cards could not stay intact for long in a household containing Mikey.

'What's that?' Perry asked, hoisting himself on to the stile. When he was settled, Clare handed it to him.

A man with a staff in one hand, the other gripping a bundle on a stick, was making his way across what looked like an ill-prepared beet-field. A dog was clawing at his rump, and seemed already to have destroyed his breeches. Beneath was written: LE MAT. THE FOOL.

'Mikey,' Clare said. 'He must have slipped it into my pocket. His way of telling me I'm a charley.'

'That's my card,' Perry said, studying it gravely.

'Yours?' Clare said. 'Do you mean because you're called Matt?'

'No,' Perry said. 'The Fool is the Wild Man. Therefore me.'

And he could be, too, thought Clare, surveying him. A wild man's smile. A wild man's elsewhere-looking eyes.

'You also have a card,' Perry said. 'I'll tell you some day what it is. May I keep this?'

Clare shrugged his assent, and Perry slipped it into his pocket. Out of the sky, invisible, a bird was singing. It brought to Clare a memory of Malkin. A chirruping, a lilting, a celebration. The English countryside, he reflected, was so insistently literary. As if following his thought, Perry murmured: 'Hark, hark, the lark.' He twisted about on the stile, and looking at the far bold flag, added: 'Yes, indeed; happy birthday, Shakespeare.'

Clare, lying sleepless, heard Perry's bedroom door open, then sensed a stir of his own door, which was ajar. He switched on his lamp, and saw Perry's head looking in at him.

'What's up?' he asked. 'That bed too hard for you?'

'I drank too much beer,' Perry said, 'or not enough. There's a highly intelligent graffito in the bog of that pub of yours. It says: "You don't buy the beer here, you rent it."'

He roamed from window to window, looking out at the moonlit wood, the moonlit field. He was wearing only his cavalry twills. It gave Clare gooseflesh to watch him.

'Didn't you even get as far as putting on your pyjamas?'

'What pyjamas?' Perry said. 'I took the trouble to pull on

some trousers, in case you should leap out of the window and break a leg.'

'Uh-huh,' Clare muttered. 'Matt, that subject doesn't make me laugh.'

'I like to set your teeth on edge,' Perry confessed. 'Sorry, I eat dirt.' He came to sit on the end of the bed. 'Your friend John and I had a jolly evening.'

'He was impressed,' Clare said, 'that you beat him at darts.'

'I play a lot,' Perry said, and looked enigmatic. Clare had a vision of rough and packed city pubs, like one he had strayed into near Spitalfields, where a friendly regular had told him he would not find it quite his style. On Perry's forearm, he noticed, there was an elaborate tattoo. A snarling dragon was coiled about a screaming eagle.

'That must have hurt,' he said, pointing at it.

'Not much,' Perry said. 'I've another one.' He twisted his arm, and Clare saw near the crook of the elbow a star of David.

'Why that?' he asked.

'Solidarity. In memory of Auschwitz. Did you know I'm a Jew?'

'You!' Clare exclaimed. 'Ah, come off it, Matt.'

'I am,' Perry said quietly.

'But — ' Clare began to say.

'You mean I was no different from anyone else at school. But one can be C. of E. and a Jew. My mother was. Her parents, and my father too, had this urge to belong.'

'Then you do belong,' Clare said. 'You don't *look* Jewish, not remotely.'

'Innocent old C.C.,' Perry remarked. 'In a moment you'll be telling me I haven't a Jewish accent.'

'Well,' said Clare, uncertainly, 'it doesn't seem to matter. Except to you, apparently.'

'And my parents,' Perry said. 'You see, the Hitler-time made them have a lot of second thoughts. And then there was Israel. My father feels very involved with Israel. And wants me, one of these days, to marry a Jewish girl. I probably shall.'

73

'From the way you've been talking,' Clare said, 'I didn't foresee marriage.'

Perry said: 'For a student of the science of man, there are an awful lot of books, old Clare, that have been closed to you.'

In the trees outside a roosting pheasant honked, and Perry flinched at the sound. 'The eerie noises here,' he said. 'Owls, and pheasants, and I heard something I thought was a fox. Don't you get the jimjams all alone down here?'

'No,' Clare said. 'Down here was what I wanted.'

'Clare,' Perry said, leaning nearer to him. His eyes in the lamp's weak light were North Sea grey. 'I came in here for a reason. Let's have a talk, Clare.'

'What about?' Clare asked guardedly.

'About you. I met a man on leave from out where you were. He told me as much as he knew.'

The tension began in Clare's neck and spread downwards. Suddenly all his miseries came back, with memories of endless nights when he had lain as if crucified in the double-beds of foreign hotels, his arms outstretched, his body almost arched with rigidity. The freedom he had snatched, against advice, had been in fact a torment of insomnia, broken by nightmares in his fits of sweating sleep.

'Matt,' he said, his voice cracking, 'I can't. Can't talk. I'd burst into tears, and you'd wish you'd never started it.'

'Have you?' Perry asked. 'Have you cried?'

'In the hospital. When they tried to make me talk about it.'

'Try now,' Perry said. 'See how it feels.'

Clare was already crying. Perry's arms went around him, and he cried on Perry's bare shoulder, unashamed, inexhaustibly.

'Now tell me why,' Perry said, into his ear. 'Cris. Why did you try to hang yourself?'

'I thought I was mad,' Clare said, choking. 'I *was* mad, at the time.'

'That's bullshit,' Perry said, holding him close. 'That much I do know. You had malaria, because you were a fool and hadn't stocked up with drugs.'

'Half-true,' Clare admitted. He had ceased to weep. 'It was the first time. I didn't know what it was, and it was frightening. Also I had malnutrition, which does something. And then there was what they called in the hospital a delayed mourning reaction. But it was worse than that. In the hospital they asked whether I heard voices. I didn't, not imaginary ones, but I did imagine – conspiracies.' He stuttered on the next word. 'Calumnies. People talking too fast and too low for me to understand. And they were all I had. I'd lost the feeling of being a white man. They were all I had.'

'And now,' Perry said, 'what will happen? You're better, I think. That level-headed little Lucy said so, and I'd believe her.'

'It's true,' Clare said, 'I do feel it. In a little while I'll go into a hospital in London for tests. Liver and spleen and so on, but mainly a test for brain damage. They're sure there is none, but they want me to be sure.'

He tried to pull away, but Perry would not release him. 'Tell me what happened that night on the island.'

'I can't,' Clare said. He was crying again, not sobbing, merely melting. 'Let it be, Matt.'

'There was a storm, this man I met had heard.'

'There was a storm,' Clare repeated. 'Dear God, what a storm. I was excited. I felt strong, potent, in some way. I hadn't felt like that for so long. I thought I would do something, be decisive. Put an end to it, remove myself, because nothing else was wrong there, only me.'

'And then?' Perry prompted.

'There's no privacy there. Never, at any hour of the day. I was followed. Daibuna – a friend of mine – he'd never heard of such a thing, never seen a sight like it. But he knew what to do. He cut me down with this bushknife.'

There might have been some prowler in the wood, for wakened pheasants suddenly burst out in a cacophony of alarm, and the two young men, one clasping the other like a wounded soldier, started apart at the demonic sound, and looked to the window as if for real demons which might be hovering there.

Clare lay back on his pillow, his eyes on Perry's face. His own face was calm, wept-out. His hand rested on Perry's, then travelled up the forearm to the tattoed star. 'Plenty of worse things have happened,' he said. 'Oh, but to be so cut adrift. Perhaps even the German Jews didn't quite know that.'

'You feel better, C.C.,' Perry asked or stated, turning on him his eyes of North Sea grey.

'So much, Matt. It's funny. I don't even feel ashamed about weeping all over you.'

'You see, I am good for something.'

'Yes,' said Clare. 'Yes, Matt, you're very good.'

He wondered at the protectiveness, the paternal streak, in so young a man. It was perhaps Perry's intense, unalloyed maleness which was at the root of what he would not see as a problem.

'We won't mention it again,' Perry promised. He stood up, clutching his bare hairy torso with long arms. 'I must leave you now, this minute.'

'Cold?' Clare said. 'I'm not surprised.'

'Cold nothing,' Perry said. 'It's that wonderworking Suffolk beer. Like the man said, you rent it.'

In the churchyard, while Perry examined the headstone of the gaffer of Hole Farm, Clare lifted his head at the sudden sound of the organ. What was it about the music, the tune woven into it? He said to Perry: 'Would you mind, shall we go in?'

The chill of the church was dispelled a little by the great iron stove, still warm from the morning service. Taking the pew nearest it, Clare and Perry sat and listened to the unseen organist.

'Green,' Clare was thinking. Somehow the music was green. It elaborated itself around a tune which he could not place, something old with the word 'green' insistent in it. Folk tune or Elizabethan song – he could not remember. But he knew that he was listening to green music.

Perry, beside him, got up and wandered silently away. He disappeared round the screen which hid the organ.

When the music stopped, Clare wanted it to begin again. And so, after a few minutes, it did, and Perry came back with a complacent expression to resume his seat beside Clare.

'For you,' he murmured aside. 'Special request.'

When the music ceased for the second time, Clare asked: 'Who is it playing?'

'A girl,' Perry said. 'A blonde girl. Very blonde. I asked her for a repeat, and she just smiled, and did. The most extraordinary eyes.'

He had hardly seen her face, Clare realized, or those eyes which had been so much noticed. There had been only that glimpse on New Year's Day, on the snowy step of the Shoulder of Mutton with the light behind her.

'What is it?' he asked. 'I seem to know it. Did you see?'

'Yes,' Perry said, 'when she turned back to start again. It's by Sweelinck. Called something in Dutch.'

'It's about green,' Clare said. 'Something something green.'

'That's it,' Perry confirmed. 'The last word was "groen". Do you suppose she is Dutch?'

'It doesn't follow,' Clare pointed out. 'And the tune – the tune is English. "Green". I just can't put a name to it.'

'Look, I'll go and ask her,' Perry offered, and wandered off again towards the screen. But he came back with a mystified face, and said: 'She's vanished.'

'She could be in the vestry,' Clare suggested. 'Perhaps the vicar's there. Let's not pursue her.'

'I shouldn't mind,' said Perry, looking preoccupied. 'Pursuing her, I mean. What eyes. And a mouth like an unawakened angel.'

'Is that your fancy,' Clare said, 'to seduce an angel? Ah Matt, you worry me.'

Perry said, with his wild man's grin: 'Don't give it a thought. I'm amazingly more decent than I care to appear.'

Clare glanced at his watch. 'I suppose we'd better start walking for that train.'

Perry, picking up his opulent briefcase, said: 'While we're alone, and not walking, just a word.'

In the light from the plain glass windows (for the church had been vandalized by Puritans) his eyes were of the bleakest grey. 'You do me good,' he said.

'*I* do *you* good?' said Clare, and laughed in his surprise. But he knew what Perry meant. In his weakness, without forethought, he had found a way to comfort a man made lonely by strength.

In the dusk, walking back from the station, pausing to watch the cloudlike transformations of rushes under the breeze, Clare thought he knew what he would begin to write that night. The breeze smelt salt, sweeping up the long estuary from the sea, the bleak North Sea. *Quasi spectantibus insultans*, he thought, remembering Perry's wild grin, his changeable eyes. And as he walked along the earth dike fringed with celandine, he began from memory to rehearse the opening of the Lord Abbot's Tale. *Temporibus Henrici regis secundi cum Bartholomeus de Glanvilla custodiret castellum de Oreford, contigit . . .*

Concerning a
wild man caught in the sea

(De quodam homine silvestri in mare capto)

In the times of King Henry the Second, when Bartholomew Glanville was Constable of Orford Castle, it happened that some fishermen of that place discovered in their net a marvellous catch.

Squatting on the bucking boat on the chill autumn sea, a young soldier was trying not to think of his stomach. His open-air ploughboy's face was sallow, and his fringe of hay-coloured hair damp with sweat.

'Heave up! Heave up!' shouted big Reynold, the owner of the boat, to his men. Then to the soldier he explained: 'I don't mean you, John. That warnt a very fortunate thing to say.'

It was not indeed, and John, running for the side, puked long and painfully. As he choked, Reynold gave him a hard friendly slap on the back. 'Keep an eye on it, boy,' he advised. 'If you see a little brown ring, thass your arsehole.'

The men hauled on the net, calling to the herring: 'Swim up! Swim up!' When the rope was exhausted, they seized the meshes. Suddenly one of them yelled: 'Reynold! Oh my Christ!'

The sick young soldier was at first too absorbed in his internal miseries to pay much attention to the hubbub all around him. But Reynold's voice, sharp with bewilderment, called 'John!' and he turned with indifferent obligingness to look at the tangle of net.

81

Between and around the legs of the gaping men herring were escaping back into the sea. But the men had eyes only for what sprawled in the dank meshes, like a baby half struggled free from a shawl.

The man was of strong, was even of beautiful build. His wet brown hair was curled, as was the beard of the same colour which all but hid his fine lips. His powerful chest was shaggy, and water trickled down it to the arrow-like line of hairs leading to the bush where his sex drooped lax and large.

His face showed no expression, his eyes merely roving from one to another of the faces staring down at him. When they came to John, they paused. There was all at once a change, like a recognition, in that gaze of North Sea grey. The brown beard twitched, and then the wild man grinned, warmly, as white as shells.

Through the afternoon mist Reynold, John and the wild man walked from the haven to the mound where the great keep, in all its splendour of newness, raised its three turrets and handsome conical roof over the marshes, the forests and the sea. A basket slung on Reynold's broad back dripped saltily. The wild man's hands were bound behind him. His eyes, though taking in everything, seemed incapable of surprise, and he walked easily, athletically, unconcerned. The great height of the keep impressed him no more than the fact of his capture out at sea.

On the steps leading up to the door, under the raised portcullis, a young sentry was standing. Peering into the mist, he said: 'That you, John? Proper boony, innit?'

'Iss,' said John. 'Me and Reynold Fisher. And another chap.'

The three passed into the vestibule, and the sentinel started and stared. 'Fucking hell,' he said. 'Who's that?'

The wild man looked at the young sentry, and his sea-grey gaze grew fixed. The soldier was a dark youth, comely in a gypsy fashion, with long-cut black eyes and a shapely, thin-

82

lipped mouth. There was humour in the mouth and the eyes, but humour which seemed to visit rather furtively. The wild man edged away from him, drawing closer to John.

'He don't like you, Robin,' John said.

'Fucking hell,' the sentry said again. 'He's bollock-naked.'

'He's a wild man,' big Reynold explained. 'Our chaps net him in the sea.'

'Fucking hell,' said Robin, for the third time. 'What are you going to do with him?'

'Take him to the Constable,' John said. 'Do you know where he's likely to be?'

'In the lower hall,' Robin said, and the flicker of a smile moved his secretive mouth. 'Yeh, you take him up there, boy.'

John and Reynold, the wild man between them, went single file up the steps, and entered the great round hall, where at the great table the Constable sat. He was in conversation with a second lieutenant, a leggy youth whose bony face had not yet settled into adulthood. They paid no attention to the new arrivals, but somebody else had done so. From the stone bench encircling the room there came a feminine cry.

'Lucy! Amabel!' commanded the Constable's lady, 'close your eyes, both of you.'

'Oh my God,' burst out the youthful officer, and seizing his cap from the vast table he rushed to hold it over the wild man's privities.

The wild man looked at him with slight puzzlement, but with unchanging calm.

'Private Westoft,' said the Constable, grimly, 'perhaps you would care to explain what you mean by coming in here with that madman, and exhibiting him to my wife and two little girls.'

'Please, sir,' John said, 'I'm very sorry, sir. I warnt aware, sir, there was ladies present. He's a wild man, sir. Reynold Fisher here, he net him in the sea.'

'How frightfully interesting,' the Constable's lady said, and she rose from the bench and came to examine the wild man, now made decent by the lieutenant's cap.

'A wild man,' said the Constable. 'I see. Does he speak?'

'No, sir,' said John. 'I mean to say, he int spoke yet.'

'And he lives in the sea?' the Constable inquired.

'It seem so, sir,' said Reynold Fisher. 'A matter of three mile out he was.'

'I see,' said the Constable again. 'That is useful to know. In a situation of marine warfare, he could be of considerable value to us.'

'Mr Clare,' said the lady to the young officer, 'your gallant work with that cap must be tiring you, and it does look just a little silly.' Turning, she called: 'Lucy, go into the kitchen, darling, and ask Mrs Kersey if she can somehow lay her hands on a pair of trousers.'

The brown girl went out, and the little fair girl who had been sitting beside her came further into the room.

'Amabel,' the lady said, 'just step upstairs to the chaplain's chamber and ask him if he would join us.'

The fair hair girl nodded and went away up the spiral stair.

'Alicia, my love,' remarked the Constable, 'what an efficient Constable you are.'

'Oh, pooh,' said the lady. 'If it takes a woman to see that Mr Clare is making himself look a perfect idiot, then it's a good thing there's a woman there.'

The brown girl came back in a hurry, and handed her mother a faded pair of blue jeans. On the fly was sewn a yellow patch, bearing the inscription: DOWN WITH PANTS.

'Now, Lucy,' the lady said, 'you and I will turn our backs, and the gentleman will do what gentlemen do in the mornings.'

The lieutenant removed the cache-sexe of his cap, wondered what to do with it, and at length clapped it on his sandy head.

'He seems very quiet and amiable,' said the Constable. 'Is there any point in having his hands bound?'

'No, sir,' said Reynold Fisher. 'Just a precaution, like.' Putting down his basket, he produced a knife from his pocket and cut the cord of the wild man's wrists.

The youthful lieutenant looked doubtfully from the jeans to the wild man. As he foresaw, what lay ahead was a complicated manoeuvre, involving first lifting one of the man's hairy legs, then the other. While this proceeded, the wild man had what looked like a fit of giggles, except that he made not the faintest sound.

At last he stood decorous before them, clothed from the navel like a Christian.

A quick step was heard on the spiral stair, and the chaplain entered, followed by Amabel. The chaplain was a big man, still youngish, black-clad and serious. But when the wild man looked at him, when he smiled in his brown beard, the chaplain smiled back with a fraternal condescension.

'He like you padre,' John said. 'I can tell. Some people he don't like one bit, but he like you and me.'

'And who,' asked the priest, 'might he be? Some poor creature weak in his wits, no doubt.'

'A wild man, padre,' said the Constable. 'Reynold Fisher caught him in the sea.'

'A wild man,' said the priest thoughtfully. 'And in the sea. Now that raises an interesting question, or confusion. A wild man is properly a man of the woods, or in Latin *homo silvestris*.'

'Silvester!' exclaimed the lady. 'But that of course, is what we must call him.' She curtsied to the wild man. 'Your servant, Master Silvester.'

'He can't be a man of the woods,' the Constable said. 'Reynold caught him three miles out. What *is* a wild man, anyway?'

'A complex business,' said the priest. 'I myself would be inclined to say that a wild man is a person of weak intellect, possibly abandoned by his parents in some wild place as a child, and therefore growing up like an animal. It is not impossible that such a man should be a powerful swimmer, could literally swim like an otter. This man may have been such an abandoned child. I notice that he breathes air quite naturally. Did it seem to you that he could also breathe in the sea?'

'I couldn't properly say,' said Reynold. 'I thought he was swimming like a man, dint you, John?'

'Couldn't say, mate,' said John. 'I was too sick to see.'

'Another possibility,' continued the priest, 'is that he is a malignant spirit inhabiting the body of a drowned man. We read of such a case in the Life of Saint Ouen.'

'He int,' said John indignantly.

'Mind your manners, soldier,' said Lieutenant Clare.

'And yours, padre,' said the lady. 'I'll not have you saying that our very pleasant-looking guest Silvester is some demon inside a corpse.'

'There remains,' said the chaplain, 'the possibility that he is a merman. I must do some reading on that, but it seems the likeliest explanation.'

'A merman!' cried the girl Lucy. 'Oh Marco — I mean, Mr Clare — would you sing us the ballad of the merman?'

'I'm afraid, Miss Lucy,' said the youth, 'this is not quite the place. But at another time, with pleasure.'

Logs were burning in the great stone-hooded fireplace, but the three large windows were growing black. The merman began to glance at them repeatedly, with unease. He drew closer to John. At length he took John's hand, and gazed into his eyes beseechingly.

'You know what I think it is,' John said. 'I think he don't like the dark. Do you suppose, sir, we could give him a place to kip?'

'With no trouble at all,' said the Constable, 'but there is the matter of security. This man is potentially a devastating weapon against the King's enemies. I'm afraid it will have to be the dungeon.'

'With a brazier,' the lieutenant said, 'the dungeon could be made quite habitable. Not that the man seems to feel the cold. But somebody should probably stay there with him.'

'Wish to volunteer, sir,' said John.

'Good show,' said the Constable. 'Organize a brazier, Mr Clare, and clean straw for both of them. Has the man eaten? Has anybody seen him eat?'

'Yes, sir,' said Reynold Fisher. 'He had a bite about eleven o'clock time. I've got his supper with me in here.'

He stooped to his basket, and took out a fine herring, which he gave to the wild man.

The wild man held it between his hands and crushed it. The juices dripped on to the stone floor. When the fish was a pulp, he wolfed it, bones, head and all.

'I should say a merman, definitely,' observed the priest.

Reynold offered another fish, and the merman dealt with it in the same way. A third was refused, with a shake of the head and a smile.

Amabel, who had not spoken until then, said in a precise little voice: 'He has a very *nice* face.' At her tone, the wild man turned and directed his smile towards her, white and warm.

'Well, Silvester,' said the lieutenant, diffident with the name, 'I'll conduct you to your quarters, and Private Westoft will see you settled.'

'Goodnight, Silvester,' said the gracious lady.

'Goodnight, Silvester,' echoed Lucy and Amabel.

The wild man hesitated. Then, awkwardly, he bent his head. It was almost a bow. He swung about, lithe and swift on his bare feet, and walked silently away after the lieutenant and John.

Later that evening the lady sat before the fire, her daughter on one side of her, her ward on the other. On a stool a few yards away sat the lieutenant, tuning his guitar.

'Well, Miss Lucy,' he said, 'here is your request. The name of it is "Annis and the Merman".'

Strumming chords, he began to sing, in a light true voice which sounded very young.

By Orwell Bridge as Fair Annis passed,
— *Ah, the sighing and the singing*
A merman rose from the deeps so vast
— *While the bells of England were ringing.*

'Oh hear me, Annis, oh hear me, pray:
Would you be my true-love, for ever and aye?'

'I wool, I wool, if rich you be,
In your own country, beneath the sea.'

He stopped her mouth, he took her hand,
He led her down to his own drowned land.

Eight years they bode, eight years together,
And seven sons called the merman father.

Annis sat by the cradle and sang.
The bells of England, how sweet they rang.

Annis stepped to the merman's door:
'To church, to church let me goo once more.'

'You shall, dear heart, you shall this day,
Till your children call you, and then away.

'But once you pass by the churchyard wall,
Your yellow hair you must not let fall.

'And once you tread on the flagstones bare,
You must turn aside from your mother's chair.

'The priest will speak the Sacred Word.
You must not kneel nor bow your head.'

He stopped her mouth, he took her hand,
He led her forth to the English strand.

When Annis passed by the churchyard wall,
Her yellow locks, she let them fall.

And when she trod on the flagstones bare,
She turned her straight to her mother's chair.

The priest spoke out the Sacred Word,
And deep she kneeled, and bowed her head.

'Oh hear me, Annis, me own first born:
Where was you, gal, all them years I mourn?'

'Eight year, eight year in the marman's hall,
And his seven sons, I bear them all.'

'Oh tell me, Annis, me darest darter:
What give the marman to be your suitor?'

'A band of gowd so red and fine
The Queen's hand haint none sich as mine.

'A pair of gowden-buckled shoes
The Queen can cry for do she choose.

'A harp of gowd, for me to sing
When me heart was sick with sorrowing.'

The merman made him a broad broad road
From shingle strand to the chapel yard.

At the chapel threshold he entered in;
The images turned away from him.

His hair was of the purest gold,
His eyes they were so sorrow-filled.

'Oh hear me, Annis, what I shall say:
Your children call you, and still you stay.'

De quodam homine silvestri in mare capto

'Let them, let them, if call they must.
They oont lie no more on their mammy's breast.'

'Oh think of the big lads, think of the small,
Think of the pitman,* the least one of all.'

'I oont think no more of the big nor the small'
— Ah, the sighing and the singing
'And least of the pitman, the least of them all'
— While the bells of England were ringing.

The dungeon was a pit, twelve feet square, twelve feet high. In the daytime it was lit by one narrow window, but that night there was only the glow from the brazier near the ladder leading to the floor above. It was close, damp and malodorous from the garderobe nearby, but for once it was warm, and the straw bedding was fresh and sweet.

As John rattled the poker in the brazier, a sharp small face looked down from overhead. The porcine eyes of Corporal Snart were on the wild man, who suddenly drew back, and going to the darkest corner, buried himself in straw.

Under a bristling nicotine-stained moustache, Snart bared yellow teeth. 'So that's him, is it? Seem to me he stink like a trawler.'

'What you smell is piss,' said John angrily, 'from the fucking garderobe. He smell a fucking sight sweeter than some people I could name, and that int so very surprising, seeing he wash himself twenty-four hours a day.'

'He don't talk, they tell me,' the corporal remarked.

'No, he don't,' John said. 'Pity that int infectious.'

'I shan't be surprised,' said the corporal mysteriously, 'if he do talk, one of these days.'

When the corporal was gone, John went and lay in the straw. From his shirt he produced a little box, and placed it

pitman: 'The last child of a family, or the smallest of a brood or litter.' Moor's *Suffolk Words and Phrases* (1823).

90

between himself and the wild man. When he had turned a knob, it began to make music.

'Thass a good radio, that,' John said. 'Got that cheap in Aden, I did, when I come home from Malaya.'

The wild man was enchanted, was rapt. The disc-jockey's voice made him grin with delight. A look sentimental almost to tears was on his face as he listened to the winner of the Eurovision Song Contest.

'Good old Luxembourg,' John said. 'Thass always there. But it's lights out time, dear boy.' He switched off the transistor and burrowed into the straw. 'Goodnight, Silvester.'

Half an hour later, John's snoring was stopped by the sound of Pearl Bailey. He rolled over, and found that the wild man had discovered the secret of the on-switch. He turned it off, took the wild man's hand and slapped it. 'Bad,' he said, and went back to sleep.

Not long afterwards he was wakened again. A hand was pressing his hand, and pressing it to warm hairy flesh.

'Oh Jesus, Silvester,' cried John, 'you int one of them, are you?'

But by the dim glow of the brazier he saw what it was. The wild man, who appeared to be clasping John's hand tenderly to his cheek, was in fact listening to his wristwatch.

In the daytime, for the sake of his health, the wild man would be taken by John to one or other of the three turrets. From here they would look down on the church and village and the river with its boats; or over the marshes to the vague blue water and the misty loom of Orford Ness; or across the fields to the darkness of Tunstall forest. The wild man looked, saw everything, but showed nothing in his face.

He was taken to the chapel, a pretty room, only marred by the graffito of some bored or pious soldier, who had printed on the wall: SUDDEN PRAYERS MAKE GOD JUMP. In the chapel he showed no sign of reverence, ignoring the images, merely staring puzzled at head-bowings and genuflections. The chaplain, who had had thoughts of preparing him for baptism, abandoned them.

One night, while John was on guard in a turret and the wild man lay, as he always did as soon as night fell, in his straw, two clumsy figures climbed down a ladder into the dungeon. They were Corporal Snart and Robin, and both were drunk. They also chinked with hidden bottles, and Robin was carrying a rope.

The wild man sat up in the straw and watched them, grey-eyed. He did not look afraid, but to Corporal Snart he conveyed fear most intensely, and the corporal was gratified.

'How do, Silvester,' he said. 'I believe the time has come for us to have a little conversation.'

The wild man began to leap up, but Robin bore him down on the straw. With the cord and a knife the corporal bound his wrists. Then he tied his ankles, and rose holding the long remnant of rope.

'Give us a bunk-up, boy,' he said. And when he was on Robin's shoulders, he contrived to sling the rope over a hook in the vault.

The wild man was slowly hauled by his ankles from the straw. He hung upside-down, his trailing hair just brushing the stone floor.

'So you don't go in for talking,' said the corporal, lighting a cigarette. 'Well, thass very interesting, scientifically. For my peace of mind I should rather like to know what kind of noise a merman make.'

He approached his cigarette-end to the wild man's armpit. There was a stench of hair, and then of burning flesh.

When Robin stooped to look at the wild man's face, he saw that his teeth were set in a straight white grin.

'Nothing to say?' asked the corporal. 'Well, we got plenty of time. One thing I don't like, Silvester, and thass foreigners swamping the country. I mean, wild men and mermen and such – what are they doing here? Thass what Sir Oswald Mosley say, and he's a proper educated gent, and married into a family that's right ubiquitous. I went to Capetown once, and it was full of fucking niggers. It int right. And I don't like you hanging there, Silvester, wearing our English britches, when you know you never sin a pair of britches before you leave that undersea slum where you was spawned. So I think, Silvester, I'm going to have them English britches off you. Yes,' said the corporal, producing a knife, 'I claim them for the King.'

The merman hung naked, the slashed jeans on the floor by his dangling hair.

'Well, Silvester,' said the corporal, puffing at his cigarette, 'it do seem that you burn like a human being. But a human being, it appear to me, ought to speak English. So I'm going to give you a little lesson in English, Silvester. I do hear there int nothing make a man speak English so fluent as a lighted fag-end on the goolies.'

When the fire bit into his scrotum the wild man screamed. But the scream was quite silent.

Robin, his face unreadable, swigged off the last of his barley wine. He stood studying the pretty label.

'Give me that,' said the corporal, reaching out. 'Less see how he like a bottle up his bottle.'

With the brown glass protruding from his anus, the wild man screamed continuously. His mouth was a great pink cave behind his white teeth. But out of that cave no sound emerged.

The corporal came from behind him and squatted to see his face. With his rump turned towards the wild man, he put down his head to see him right way up.

There was suddenly a tearing sound. Through a rent in the corporal's trousers, the wild man's teeth were sunk into his buttock.

The corporal sprang up, bleeding. He rushed to the brazier, and rammed the poker into the coals.

93

'Er — corp,' Robin said. 'No, boy.'

But the furious, pig-eyed corporal swung about with the glowing poker.

From the floor many feet above him John launched himself into air. He staggered, but recovered. His sword was in his hand.

'Drop that, Snart,' he said. 'If you don't, I shall have your fucking hand off.'

The corporal raised the poker, but the nearness of the sword made him think again. He threw the poker with a clang on to the stone floor under the brazier.

'Something tell me, Private Westoft,' he said, 'reading the tea-leaves, like, that there might be a court-martial in the offing.'

John's hot face and blazing blue eyes, his generous fury, made him almost handsome. 'I should wholly enjoy that,' he said. 'Then me and the Constable might have a little chat. Like about why young Harry Bury have a nervous breakdown and get invalided out.'

The corporal's expression became fiercely still. 'What do you mean, Westoft?'

'What I mean,' John said, 'is I know what happen to Harry Bury. That you and that fucking sergeant hold his head down the fucking garderobe while you bugger him. Thass what I mean.'

'Hey, John,' Robin said. 'Easy, John.'

'And you int much fucking better,' John said. 'I don't know what's the matter with you. If you hang about with this turdburglar much longer you'll end up as big a cunt as what he is.'

'Hey, John,' Robin said again.

'Piss off,' John said. 'This is our place, Silvester's and mine. If you int up that ladder in five seconds you shall find yourself with a hole in a surprising place.'

The dark youth went, but the corporal hovered bristling

at the foot of the ladder. 'I int finished with you, Westoft.'

'Thass kind of inconvenient,' John said, 'because I never been so finished with anybody as you. My advice to you, Snart, is stick your National Front up your national backside. If it come to reading tea-leaves, I can do a bit of that myself. What England's going to do to you lot is what Silvester do to raw fish, and that won't be pretty, but by Christ, I shall laugh like a drain. And don't you forget, Snart, fatal accidents happen in the Army, even to NCOs.'

The corporal looked again at the sword, and went in furious silence, at a dignified speed, up the ladder.

With his sword John hacked through the rope binding the wild man's wrists. When the wild man could stand on his hands, John freed his feet and helped him to the straw.

The wild man's face had no expression, but on each cheek was one tear, as still as if frozen.

'That was bad,' John muttered, flopping beside him. 'That was bad, Silvester.' He dug into the straw for his transistor and switched it on.

The wild man sat up, and put a hand on John's right ankle.

'You don't miss much,' John said, 'I'll say that for you, Silvester. Yeh, I sprain it, I reckon.' He watched the wild man's clever fingers unlace his boot, and felt the strong hairy fingers massaging.

Suddenly he rolled on his side and switched the wireless to full volume.

'Sorry, lads,' the disc-jockey was saying, 'not Awful, I meant to say *Orford* Castle, where we have a request from Private John Westoft, hullo there, John, who wants us to play a number for his friend Silvester, hullo there, Silvester, and it's not so young as it was, but oh so true, so here for you, Silvester, with cheers from John, sung by the original cast of *South Pacific*, here's "There Is Nothing Like A Dame".'

The wild man had recognized the name of Orford, and his

own name, and John's. He listened with eyes wide and intent, his lips parted over his teeth, while automatically his fingers worked on John's ankle. When the music ended, he sighed without a sound.

'Well, Silvester and John,' said the disc-jockey, 'over there in Orford Castle, I hope that didn't give you any ideas, and if it did, well, mind how you go. Now we have a card from André Dupont in Brussels . . .'

John turned the volume down again, and looked at the wild man with huge satisfaction. 'Well,' he said, 'that wipe away the tears, dinnit?'

The wild man's face was anguished with silence. Never before had he so visibly ached to speak. He lifted John's foot and bent his head and kissed it.

'Oh shit,' John said, jerking his leg away. He switched off the transistor. 'Right, that's it. Lights out.'

The wild man rustled across the straw and lay down at a discreet distance. He turned his back on John and curled up like a miserable foetus.

'Fucking Army,' John muttered. 'Oh, this fucking Army.'

The nearness of that hurt presence, whose emotions he could so often divine, oppressed him. He said: 'Thass all right, Silvester. I mean, different countries, they have different customs. I mean, if General De Gaulle kiss me, I wouldn't dial 999. Ah, the hell with it,' he concluded his argument, and reaching out an arm tousled the wild man's hair. 'I'd sooner have you than a golden Labrador, straight up I would. Goodnight.'

Not long afterwards Corporal Snart died of tetanus. The cause, it was given out, was sitting down upon a wholly unforeseeable wool-comb.

The chaplain, though he had established no closer relationship with the wild man than a genial silence, continued to seek him out, in the dungeon or on one of the turrets to which he was escorted daily to take the air. Standing beside him one day on the west turret, watching how the man's eyes dwelt on the sea, he murmured: 'Yes, Silvester, I know no reason why you should not sometimes enjoy that element which is yours, after all.'

In the evening the chaplain went to the upper hall, where the Constable and his family had ordained a blaze against the autumn chill. 'I should like,' he said, taking the stool which they cordially offered to him, 'to discuss the merman, for I am sure now that that is what he is.'

'You have discovered something new?' asked the Constable's lady.

The priest opened a book on his black knee, and ran an eye over the lines of his own meticulous writing. 'I have discovered,' he said, 'the case of Nicholas Pipe.'

'Pipe,' repeated the Constable. 'Odd sort of name for a merman.'

'The name,' said the priest, 'is possibly a corruption of *Piscis*, or fish, though Papa is also heard. This very recent case is reported from the realm of King William II of Sicily. He was a man exactly like any other man in all his members, but for a month or a year he could live under the sea with the fish, without breathing, yet unharmed. He was a great friend to sailors, and when he sensed a storm he would warn them not to leave harbour, or if they were already at sea would urge them to put back. He asked nothing of them in return but gifts of oil, to enable him, when he was on the surface, to peer into the depths. An odd thing, which my informant does not understand, is that when he was going undersea to make a long stay he would take with him pieces of iron torn from carts, or horse-shoes, or worn-out pots from kitchens.

'At the request of the King he once descended into the whirlpools of Scylla and Charybdis, and reported that under the sea in that place was a great deep, with mountains and valleys, woods and fields, and trees bearing acorns. Though I have no reason which I could defend, I believe that that place was his own kingdom, and a rich one, and poor only in iron, which he therefore begged from the men on land.

'One peculiarity of Nicholas Pipe, or Cola Pesce, is that he could not live out of sight and smell of the sea. When he was taken any distance from it, his breath seemed to fail him. And this characteristic had, I grieve to say, tragic consequences. Not long ago King William, wanting to show him to an important guest, ordered him to be brought to court. The unfortunate Cola resisted, with the result that soldiers dragged him away by force, and in consequence of his separation from the sea he died in their hands.'

'Oh, poor Cola Pesce,' murmured Lucy.

'Our own merman,' continued the priest, 'looks continually at the sea with the greatest yearning. I myself, bearing in mind the case of Cola, have no doubt that he could speak if he chose. What is required from us, I believe, is a mark of particular kindness, confidence and friendship. I therefore suggest that Silvester, as Dame Alicia has so imaginatively named him, be given the freedom of the haven.'

The Constable gazed among the blazing logs, and thought. 'There is, of course,' he remarked, 'the security angle. The man's possible usefulness to the King is incalculable. But yes, padre, I shall give the matter my fullest consideration. And,' he added, with a wry glance aside, 'it goes without saying, Dame Alicia's.'

On a misty morning Reynold the Fisher's preparations were complete. Below the village, attached to stout poles, a triple line of nets cut off the haven from the sea.

Every inhabitant of the castle, except for two sentries, went in procession to the water. The Constable was there, with his lady and Lucy and Amabel. Before them, between John and big Reynold Fisher, walked the wide-eyed merman.

98

At the water's edge, the three got into Reynold's little boat. When the big man had rowed to mid-channel, and rested on his oars, the merman stood up and looked at John with a puzzled, beseeching grin.

'Thass okay, Silvester,' John said, and gave his bosom-friend a light shove. With scarcely a splash, the merman vanished.

He was gone a long time, and when he emerged once more he was between the first net and the second. A roar of disapproval, and of discomfiture, went up from the soldiers.

'There seems,' remarked the Constable to the second lieutenant, 'to have been a cock-up.'

'Come back, Silvester,' John bawled from the boat. 'You int supposed to be there.'

Supporting himself with one hand on the first net, the merman smiled joyously at the spectators, and gave them a two-fingered sign.

'Well, really,' murmured the Constable's lady, standing with the chaplain on the drab, misty shore.

'Other lands, other manners,' observed the priest apologetically.

'I say, Silvester,' John yelled, red-faced, 'that int very nice, boy.'

With his white, elated grin, the merman repeated the sign to his friend, and submerged.

He next appeared between the second net and the third. Then he was beyond the third net, swimming freely among the flotilla of little boats which had turned out to watch him.

To every shout, to every objurgation, he returned the same grin and the same two-fingered sign.

The chill day wore on. The military returned to the castle. Then the fishermen gave up, and went to their moorings. Only Reynold and John were left.

'Well, thass it,' said John, with a heavy face. 'He's gone.'

'Come and have a drink,' Reynold said. 'I know what it is, I been in the Army myself. You make a friend, then you lose him. Thass Army life.'

'I don't seem to fancy it,' John said. 'No, thank you, boy, I'm orfft.'

When he went to the dungeon to retrieve his radio from its hiding place in the straw John felt like crying, and did go so far as to sniff.

It was after nine at night, when Roger, who had formerly been John's best friend, was on guard inside the portcullis, that that taciturn man was shocked into words. 'Well, I'll be buggered,' he said, and began to shout.

In the great hall, hearing the commotion below and the raising of the portcullis, the Constable got up irritably from before the fire and went to the head of the steps. 'What's going on down there?' he demanded. 'Soldier – is that you, Westoft? – what's all this racket?'

But John said nothing, merely bounded up the steps into the hall. Close behind him, still glistening from the sea, was the merman.

'Silvester!' exclaimed the Constable's lady. 'So you've rejoined us.' And she and the little girls came to welcome him. But though his nudity seemed to pass unnoticed with them, there was nevertheless a slight coolness in the air, and the merman, sensing it, let the white grin die in his wet beard. The two-fingered sign had not been forgotten by Dame Alicia.

Nor was the Constable altogether forgiving. The brazier was taken from the dungeon that night, the ladder raised, and John no longer slept there. About that, John was in two minds. He knew his old bedfellow's fear of being abroad after dark, and better than anyone else understood what it had cost him to return. But the insulting gesture made towards himself had caused him offence far deeper than the lady's, and he thought that the merman needed a lesson in manners.

So the merman from that time lay alone in the straw, which was never changed. Sometimes his fingers moved as if he were

100

enjoying a tune from the radio. Sometimes he heaped up straw in the shape of his friend's sleeping body, and before sleeping himself he patted its head.

There came a day when John and Roger had leave in Wood-bridge, and at the proper time Roger returned alone. To inquiries about Private Westoft, the silent older soldier merely said that he had 'lorst 'im'.

John returned two days late. Taken before the Constable, his only explanation was: 'She was worth it.'

'I hope you'll continue to think so,' said the Constable. 'Mr Clare, make arrangements for that man to be flogged.'

The flogging took place below the mound, before all the castle's company. Among them was the merman. His face showed no expression, but on each cheek was one unmoving tear.

That night John came back to the now freezing dungeon, to the wet and stinking straw. John could not stop shivering. The merman prepared him a bed in the driest corner, heaped straw over him, and on top laid his own warm body, which never suffered from cold. But through the straw he felt his friend still quivering, as if in the throes of malaria.

In the dark the merman went to the wall where the ladder usually hung. His cunning fingers and toes found impossible crannies, he swarmed up the glistening wall to the level of the vestibule. The portcullis was raised, but a sentry slouched near it. With regret, with no great force, the merman gave a chop to the soldier's neck, and the man toppled. The merman caught him and lowered him carefully to the floor, where he lay still.

Going back to the dungeon, the merman let down the ladder and went to rouse John. John had not been fully asleep, but was feverish and light-headed, and could only say, as he was helped up the ladder: 'It int morning, is it?'

They wandered through a night of mist and rusty brambles,

over a field, by a windmill, across a marsh. John's thoughts were in confusion; he responded like a child to the merman drawing on his wrist, the merman supporting him.

They came to a halt, and the merman swept up his friend in his arms. The young soldier, with a laugh which sounded delirious with fatigue, muttered: 'I int a gal, mate, I can climb over a stile.'

The merman stood with his friend in his arms, and looked down sharp-eyed through the gloom. John's eyes had closed, and he burrowed into the merman's shoulder, muttering, almost asleep. A slight white smile divided the merman's beard. He leaped into the sea.

The merman entered into his own kingdom, with its vales and hills, its woods and fields, its orchards bearing acorn-shaped fruits. Among the trees rose his palace, its walls and turrets white as coral, its roofs agleam with copper and gilded vanes.

The great hall of the palace welcomed him silently as master. His grey gaze took in with a quiet joy the familiar things of his life: the Egyptian gold, the Grecian marbles, the complexities of Celtic bronze.

With a gentle movement of his shoulder he shifted the head of his human guest to lie in the crook of his arm. The merman smiled. John's mouth was slightly open, his round blue eyes were wide.

The merman bent his head and lightly, almost timidly, kissed the parted lips, the staring eyes. But John was drowned. The merman threw back his head and howled, in a great bubble of soundless grief.

MAY

In the late May light of his study, Clare sat reading a letter from Maine.

So your kind of life seems pretty suburban to me, surrounded like this by four hundred acres of woods. The stream is my kitchen sink and my shower (it's melted snow, kind of cool), and I'm writing by the light of a kerosene lamp, as close as I can huddle to a potbellied stove burning pine. Just before dark I went down to the stream to hook out a couple of cans of Narragansett (that's beer, as you wouldn't know) and found myself eyeball to eyeball with a bear on the other side. We just squatted and stared at each other, three feet apart. Right behind it was the apple tree, all in flower, that some bear planted years ago by eating an apple miles from here, and getting rid of the seeds in the usual way. They aren't all so helpful. Anything I plant or bury, like potatoes or trash, they dig up, sniff at, and leave for me to bury again.

I don't know that it's for you to say that what you're writing is too stupid to show to anyone else. But if it's therapy, well, I understand that. Me, I write poems that look like Fenimore Cooper trying to write like – who? St John Perse, maybe. He has this phrase *un grand poème délébile* – delible as opposed to indelible, get it? I write the most delible poems you'll never see.

I could stay here for ever, but soon I'm off to teach in Summer School. And in fall, it's back to Academe, for the first time in plain clothes. That will leave my brothers with a few more bucks for themselves, but I'll miss this wilderness.

Just outside the door there's a phoebe nesting. I don't guess you know what a phoebe is, but she's a little shock-headed thing. At first, she'd fly off every time I came out, but now we understand each other, and she just sits and fixes me with a beady little eye. It reminds me of you and your wren, but my phoebe's more placid and more the outdoor type.

Remember me to Alicia, Mrs K., Mark, Lucy, Mikey and that supernatural little Amabel. Also Peter at the Mutton, John, Roger and Robin. And to you,

Peace.

JIM-JACQUES

Clare put down the letter and picked up another, with an Iranian stamp. The stamp puzzled him, and the writing. He could not remember having seen it before.

The telephone rang, and with a start he lifted it. Mark Clare's voice, much noise in the background, said: 'Cris, I'm ringing from a box at Charing Cross, and I'm skint. Could you ring me back at this number?'

'Sure,' Clare said, noting the number on Jim-Jacques' letter. He broke the connection, then dialled.

'Thanks, Cris,' Mark said. 'Listen, would you do me another favour?'

'If it's as easy as that one.'

'It's a bit of a liberty. Well, a diabolical liberty. You see, there's this girl, and she's got a car, and on Saturday morning I'd like to bring her down to yours.'

'Understand,' Clare said. 'I'll make myself scarce.'

'Oh, don't put it like that. Just for a while. Suppose we stay the night? She could cook you a decent meal.'

'It depends how you want to arrange it,' Clare said. 'By the time you arrive I'll be out, anyway. I'm going to a football match in Ipswich with John and Roger. I'll see you about suppertime, if you're still here.'

'Oh well, that's great,' Mark said. 'That's really great. You won't mention it to anyone will you?'

'No, of course not,' Clare said. 'Though anyone is more broad minded than you probably know. Listen, Mark, I've got to hang up on you, someone's knocking on the door.'

He put down the receiver with a ping and went to open the door, feeling a new interest when he saw the big fair man who stood there. 'Morning, Reg.'

'Morning, master,' said Reg. 'What's your pleasure today?'

'Nothing much,' Clare said. 'The usual pair of kippers, I suppose. No, make it three. I'm expecting company, for a change.'

'Lonely old place, this,' Reg said. 'But pretty.' Moaning with pigeons, blooming with lilac, hawthorn and laburnum, the neglected garden seemed to belong to some idyllic time before nature needed to be rearranged by man.

Clare looked at the fisherman (Reynold the Fisher, he was called now in his mind) and thought that with his crisp hair, his clear eyes and single gold ear-ring, he had all the freshness of the sea upon him. 'How's business?'

'Well, that int you,' Reg said, 'that make it worth my while to come all the way from Lowestoft. But passable, thanks.'

Clare went with him to his van, which was parked on the farm road beside the stream. They walked by the apple tree, a tethered cloud of blossom fading to white. Under their feet crushed camomile smelled pharmaceutically sweet.

From the field opposite the cottage an oak leaned its bright new leaves over the van. The steep sides of the stream were a mass of cow-parsley, reaching up to the overhang of a flowering hawthorn hedge. Though buttercups and red campion were everywhere, the insistent note of the countryside was white embowered in green.

Reg handed over the fish, and climbed into the van. 'Hey, wait a minute,' Clare said, 'I haven't paid you.'

'My memory,' said the rueful fisherman, accepting the few coins. 'It get like that when you're over twenty-one. But you wouldn't know, would you? Enjoy your company.'

In the study once more, Clare slit open the letter from Iran. Inside was only a card. A Tarot card: The Hanged Man.

He felt a horror of it, of the malice which must have sealed it and addressed it. He stared at the envelope, and all at once thought that he knew the writing. From his memory of a single postcard, he believed it was Matthew Perry's.

He turned the Hanged Man over. On the back was written: *'Your card = Resurrection. M.J.P.'*

Later in the morning, while Clare was slashing weeds in the garden, surrounded by the pungency of hedge-garlic and by the Orange Tip butterflies which lived on it, the young carpenter Robin came to replace a cracked warped door. He carried the new one on his back from the van, stooped under it like a certain arthritic old farm labourer who haunted the fireplace of the Shoulder of Mutton. Below the inevitable cap of black wool, his gypsy-like eyes had their usual look of faint amusement; which, it occurred to Clare, was not exactly friendly, not exactly unfriendly, not exactly anything but detached and interested. Like a grey squirrel, thought Clare.

'Cup of tea before you start?' he asked, and Robin said: 'Wouldn't say no.'

They sat in the whitewashed back kitchen with its quarried floor, its old copper and bread-oven. 'Can't see a modern woman living here,' said Robin.

'I'm not particular,' Clare said. 'Speaking of women, Mark's found one.'

'Oh-ah,' Robin said. 'Not a bad old boy, Mark. We int the same class, of course, but we always been friends, since we was babies. Well, you tell Mark he int the only one.'

Looking at Robin's slight reminiscent smile, his secretive

108

mouth, Clare guessed that he was not speaking of courtship, of anything that touched him.

'No?' he said. 'Well, good luck, Robin.'

The gypsy-dark boy was overtaken by the urge to confide. 'You ever sin a blonde girl walking about here?'

'Yes,' Clare said. 'With green eyes?'

'Thass the one,' Robin said. 'Well, I was out in the van Monday and I see her walking along miles from anywhere and I stop and offer her a lift. Well, one thing lead to another with surprising speed. I never been raped before, and I recommend it.'

Clare found himself oddly shocked, his image of the girl violently revised. 'You don't mean that?'

'That's how it seem the first time,' Robin said. 'The other two was quite voluntary.'

The boy was grinning widely, and Clare saw in his mouth something innocently feral.

'I hope,' he said, not knowing why he should be concerned, 'you were kind to her, Robin.'

'Well, I warnt unkind,' said Robin. 'But don't you worry about her. My experience warnt a rare one, by all accounts. They say there's only three things she's interested in, and two of them are round.'

Clare wanted to change the subject, but still had a question. 'Where does she come from, did she say?'

'No,' Robin said. 'She don't go in for talking. But she's a stranger of some kind. I'd say Welsh.'

He set down his empty mug and scraped back his chair. 'Well, to work,' he said. Then, with a return of his enigmatic smile: 'Given you something to think about, haven't I?'

'Yes, you have,' Clare admitted. 'Welsh, you think? I'd never have thought of that.'

On Saturday, after the football match, Clare was dropped by John and Roger at the top of Hole Lane. An early full moon was out, and at the end of the lane he stopped to look up at the chestnut tree. In that light the tree's little pagodas of bloom were drained of their rose veining and gleamed an eggshell white.

Before going in, he skirted the cottage, but found no car. They had gone, he decided, and the light in the study had been left on to guide him home.

But in the study, before a fire stoked high against the house's pervading chill, Mark was slumped in the rickety armchair. He turned his face towards the door, and Clare was shocked by it. 'Marco! What is it?'

'Nothing much,' Mark said. 'Here, have your chair and get warm.'

'No, stay there,' Clare said, and went to lean on the mantel-piece, trying not too evidently to observe the stricken young face.

'She went,' Mark said. 'For me it wasn't a minute too soon. I told her I'd stay the night with you. I'll walk to the station in the morning.'

'Oh, Mark,' Clare said, compassionately. 'Forget about it. She's obviously a bitch.'

'It wasn't obvious,' Mark said. 'But then, I haven't had much experience in judging. One thing that's clear is that we weren't made for one another.'

He turned his head away, and began thumping on the arm of the chair with growing violence. 'But who am I to com-plain? I'm boring to look at and boring to talk to and boring in bed. I was lucky to get what I did get.'

Clare stared down into the fire, ignoring the boy's tears. Eventually Mark sniffed, and said: 'Cris.'

'Yes, Marco.'

'I brought a bottle of whisky. Couldn't afford it, but I thought it looked sophisticated. Let's get pissed, Cris.'

'That's the spirit,' Clare said. 'I'm with you to the end of the bottle.'

Much later, almost asleep, Mark asked: 'Cris?'

'Hullo?'

'Have you ever had a woman down here?'

'Not yet,' Clare said. 'But there's one I think about.'

110

'What's she like?' Mark asked drowsily.

Clare thought about what she was like. 'Green as elder-flower,' he said. 'Eyes green as elderflower.'

He wandered over to the table, where the book lay open. His eyes skimmed the familiar opening words.

Aliud quoque mirum priori non dissimile in Suthfolke contigit apud Sanctam Mariam de Wulpetes . . .

Concerning a
boy and a girl emerging from the earth

(De quodam puero et puella de terra emergentibus)

Another wonder not unlike the appearance of the wild man occurred in Suffolk at St Mary Woolpit. On the manor at this place belonging to Richard Calne, a soldier, a great throng of reapers was proceeding along the harvest field. The day was bright and hot, which, as afterwards appeared, was not without bearing on what followed; poppies and may weed stared in the yellow grain as yet unapproached by the reapers and gleaners; and over the summer-darkened hedgerows tangled with woodbine and traveller's joy, invisible larks sang.

Some way from the field, in a sandy place grown with gorse, there were certain hollows or pits, which ignorant people called the Wolf Pits, to explain to themselves the name of the village. Towards these pits, during a pause in the work, a young reaper strayed on some business of his own, and so became (with round eyes and gaping mouth) the first to observe the prodigy over which the Abbot of Coggeshall and many more have marvelled.

Crouched near the edge of one of the pits this John observed two children, whom at first he took to be the children of neighbours playing at some game; for the sun was in his eyes and they were a little shadowed by a clump of brambles. But at the sound of his feet in the gorse the children rose and looked towards him, their eyes narrowed against the light, and seeming to see him only dimly, if at all. They were a girl and boy of perhaps seven and six years old, comely in form and in every way like any children of our world. But their hair and their eyes and all their skins were of the green of leeks.

The young reaper for some minutes only stared at their fear, with fear of his own in which there was pity too. Then he turned about and ran back to the harvest field, shouting to the lord of the harvest: 'Roger! Roger, see what's here!'

In a narrow vale stood the manor house of Wikes, looking out over its fishponds to a little wood which closed the view. Built of stone, whitewashed within and without, with a steep thatched roof adapted to the line of its curved ends, the house rose with a modest ceremony out of a ceremonious garden on the same small scale. A plot of fine grass lay before the hall door, bordered by other plots of herbs and roses. At the south end a wall enclosed an orchard of pears, apples, quinces, cherries, plums and a single vine, and there the strawberries also lurked brightly. In that weather the garden and the house itself, with its open door and narrow glassless windows, moaned with the many doves from its cote throughout the day.

At the time when the children came, the knight sat in the airy hall with only his wife for company. The lady, who after many disappointments was expecting her second child, was at her spinning, though a harp was within her reach should her husband wish for cheer. For the knight was melancholy, his blue eyes shadowed, his brown beard uncombed. A wound in battle had caused him a long illness, and though a man in the prime of his age he would never fight or tourney or hunt as he had done before. By his chair there rested a stick, curiously carved, where his hand gripped, with the leafed face of the Green Man.

When the reapers descended upon the house the knight was at first too rapt in thought to attend to their noise, brooding perhaps on his wound, or perhaps, as he now often did, on his only son, a boy being educated in the household of the bishop.

116

So the lady too, for his peace, feigned to give all her attention to her spinning, though her ear was intent on the voice of Peter Butler disputing with Roger the lord of the harvest, and on the exclamations which came from Kit of Kersey, her faithful servant and friend.

At length, rising, she went some way towards the door, and called twice, not loudly: 'Kit! Oh, Kit!'

The young woman heard, and had indeed been hovering outside the door for such a call, and she came quickly, but shyly (for it was understood that at that hour the hall was the knight's alone) to her mistress. Her rosy face was a complexity of every feeling between wonder and tenderness.

'Oh Madam,' she cried. 'Oh Madam.'

'Why, Kit,' said the lady, 'how strange you look. And what is this crowd of folk in the garden? I hope it does not mean some poor soul is hurt in the harvest field.'

'Thass no wonder if I look strange,' said Kit, 'for my eyes have sin the strangest thing under the sun. Madam, they all want to come in to the master, and Peter he won't let none of them, but Madam, let Roger and John come and bring the children with them.'

'What children, Kit?' asked the lady.

'The ones John find, Madam, near the harvest field. Two children lost or strayed, but so uncommon, Madam, that it won't do no good for me to try to tell you. But have them fetched, and oh Madam, only see.'

'Tell Peter, then,' said the lady, 'that those two men and the children may enter.' And returning to her husband she said: 'The reapers have found some poor children, who are lost, it seems.'

The knight looked on idly as his sturdy butler, in a yellow tunic, marched in before the reapers. Those two, dark silent Roger and hay-haired young John, walked close together, which the knight set down to the diffidence of such men inside his house. But when the butler stopped before him, said: 'Sir, the strangers,' and stepped aside; when the knight saw what the reapers held in a manner trapped between them; then he felt like a man shocked from a long day-dream, and grasping his stick leaped up, crying: 'Holy Virgin!'

Being now out of the sun the children gazed at the knight, the most imposing man in the room, wide-eyed, and the beauty of their eyes amazed him like some stone never seen before. They were not of one unmixed green, but flecked or lined with different greens, and in each child's eyes there was a different promise; for in the boy's there was, as it were, a misting of blue, while in the girl's was a haze of pale bird-breast brown.

Nor were their skins all of a single colour, but as there is variation with us (whose arms, for example, are darker above than below), so the skins of the green children verged in some places on the fairness of ladies. Noticing this, the knight thought first of the green of leeks, where that green meets white. But his second thought was of green elderbuds, at the point where they are transfigured into bloom.

The children's hair was like silk, and green as barley, but like barley presaging gold. As for their clothes, the York-shireman William Petit has written that they were covered with raiment of unknown material; but the Abbot of Cogges-hall, who heard these things from the knight himself, says nothing of such raiment, and for good reason. For what touched the knight and his lady more than the girl's elfin face, more than the boy's little warrior's mouth and chin, was their likeness to pictures of our first father and mother before their fall. As if unaware, both covered their nakedness under small hands with nails like hazel leaves. And like our first parents, but later, both began to weep inconsolably.

That evening, when the long trestle table was set out in the hall, the green children sat not with the other children, but with the knight and his lady and with a certain priest, a true friend to the knight and himself a man of soldierly bearing, though grave. This priest looked continually at the children with wonder in which there was something of pity and of trepidation.

From all the food which was offered them, from beer and from wine, the children turned their heads away, and wept. And no delicacy prepared for them by kindly Kit, whose own child was of their age and was then in the hall, could tempt their appetite or bring a pause to their weeping.

At last the priest, who had meditated long, said to the children: '*Ydor ydorum?*' And then, touching a handsome ewer of bronze in the form of a knight on horseback, from whose horse's mouth the water poured, he added: '*Hydriai?*' But the children merely looked at the ewer and wept. And when he asked, touching the salt: '*Halgein ydorum?*' they gazed at him greenly, but evidently understood nothing, and wept again.

'What are those words, father?' inquired the knight's lady.

'I thought, Madam,' said the priest, a little discomfited, 'that in the story of the priest Elidorus there might be an answer to the marvel of these children. This Elidorus, as a boy of twelve, ran away from his studies, and hid himself in the hollow bank of a river near Neath, in Wales. And when he was in great hunger, two men of small stature came upon him and said: "If you will go with us, we shall take you to a land full of sports and delights." The boy went willingly, at first down a path under the earth which was lightless, and came at length to a most beautiful country of rivers and meadows, woods and plains, but somewhat gloomy, for the sun never shone there, nor the moon or stars. Brought to the King, he was received with wonder and with great kindness, and the King gave him into the care of his own son, also a boy.

'These men were of handsome form, with long fair hair to their shoulders like women, but very small, and their horses were the size of greyhounds. Though there was no cult of religion among them, they were strict in honour; and returning from our hemisphere, they often spoke in reprobation of our ambitions, infidelities and inconstancies, which things were unknown among them.

'The boy Elidorus soon learned their language, and was permitted to visit our world as he liked, and so came to be rejoined with his mother, to whom he told all these things. But the woman, being greedy, asked him to bring her back a present of gold from that kingdom. So, on an unlucky day, while playing at ball with the King's son, he seized the ball, which was of gold, and made off with it to his mother's house.

'But as he entered, his foot stuck fast on the threshold, and he fell. And two of those subterranean beings, following him, seized the ball, and with the greatest contempt and derision spat upon him, and he saw them no more. Nor could he ever again find the passage into their world, which was behind a waterfall, though he searched for a full year.

'Almost inconsolable, the boy took again to his studies, and at last became a priest. But even in old age he could not speak of that land and its people without tears, and their language he never quite forgot. He remembered, and told the bishop when he was well stricken in years, that *ydor ydorum* meant with them: "Bring water"; and *halgein ydorum*, "Bring salt"; and *hydriai* water-pots or ewers such as this. All these matters are told by Gerald the Welshman, and are a most powerful lesson against greed, which is the destruction of all felicity.'

'And yet, father,' said the soldier, 'these are no pygmy men, but children, and they have recognized nothing of those words remembered by the priest Elidorus.'

'My test has failed,' admitted the priest. 'And therefore I am forced back to my first position, which is that they have fallen from the moon.'

The knight and the lady said nothing to that, but the lady at length suggested: 'Let us take them into the garden, and show them the moon.'

To the moon and the stars the stubborn-faced boy paid little attention. But the girl, who seemed the older, gazed up at all the immensity above with a look of terror.

The priest spoke kindly to her, and as men will sometimes do with foreigners, made use of the one foreign tongue he knew, which was Latin. So he said, pointing: '*Luna*.' And finding that her eyes seemed to return to the red planet, he told her: '*Stella Martialis*.'

Then for the first time the child spoke. She repeated the priest's words, but strangely, so that it seemed to him that she said: '*Terra Martinianit*.' And then both children, weak with fear and hunger, began to weep again.

Some days later Kit of Kersey was passing through the hall, where the children lay on the rushes as ever in tears, carrying with her beans which her little daughter had torn roughly in the garden.

The boy, raising his head, saw the green things, and with a shout rushed at the woman, snatched the beans, and carried them to the girl. With cries they began, joyfully, starvingly, to tear at their booty, seeking the beans, however, not in the pods but in the stalks. And not finding them, they began to weep again.

But kindly Kit, forgiving the hungry child his robber's manners, came to them and showed them where the beans were to be found. And then, chattering in their unknown tongue, they eagerly devoured them, and by signs asked for more. And for a long time they nourished themselves with beans entirely.

Concerning this the priest had many doubts, for beans are condemned by Pythagoras, and are thought by some to contain departed souls. And as Bartholomew the Englishman has written: 'By oft use thereof the wits are dulled and they cause many dreams.' But the children, growing by degrees stronger and ceasing to bewail their outcast condition, became accustomed to eat whatever was set before them, and by signs made

121

the priest understand that until then they had refused other food only because of its strangeness, and from fear that it would poison them. But once their trust in Kit was firm, they would accept any dish from her hand; and from her their trust was extended to all the people of the manor, and they became happy, hearty children. But the boy was often shaken by fits of passion, and the soldier, who was growing to love him, said: 'Out of this bean will sprout a terrible knight.'

The lady's time drew near, and her son, a boy of nine years, came to visit the manor from the bishop's household where he was being schooled. And being so young, and vain of his little learning, as well as charmed by the pointed face and strange eyes of the green girl, he made a doggerel rhyme about her in Latin, calling her Viridia. And he sang it to his mother's harp.

> *Viridia mirabilis*
> *Tam pulchra quam amabilis;*
> *Colloquium nemo intelligit,*
> *Quod puto esse habilis.*

By which he meant, or wished to mean:

> Viridia the marvellous,
> As amiable as fair;
> Her speech no man can understand,
> Which shows her wit, I swear.

In due course the lady was delivered of a daughter, whom the knight welcomed with a good grace, though he had prayed for a boy, for his son Mark, he felt sure, was destined for the clergy or the court, and he longed for a little soldier. At the baptism of the child, whose name was Lucy, the green children watched intently, and the girl, pointing at the baby and at Mark, and then at herself and the green boy, made it understood that they too were brother and sister.

After that baptism the priest took to spending much time with the children, and began to teach the boy his letters, from a feeling that he might in this way come to have some knowledge of their language. The boy was no diligent scholar, having an adoration for horses and hawks, but the girl, very strangely for a female, took to learning with the ardour of a clerk, and soon not only wrote fairly, copying both English and Latin, but acquired a knowledge of our tongue, which she spoke with sometimes comical grammar, but in a clear precise accent like a lady.

So through her the priest instructed the boy in the tenets of our faith, and in time both were regenerated by the holy waters of baptism. The priest had wished to name them Barbara and Peregrine: each name, as he said, meaning 'stranger'. But because of the boy Mark's rhyme, the girl had long been called either Amabel or Mirabel, and at the lady's insistence both names were given to her at the font. As for the boy, the knight said that he was made to be a warrior, and must carry the name of the most glorious and holy of warriors, and he was therefore baptized Michael.

But not long afterwards the boy began to dwindle and pine, and when he grew too weak to walk was laid in a truckle bed in the hall, where at meal times his green eyes watched the company wistfully. He could eat little, though kind Kit brought him, in his own silver-rimmed mazer, many delicacies easy to stomach. The priest and the lady were frequently with him, and his sister always, and just as often the lame knight's chair was beside the bed. The two never spoke, but the soldier would look with a yearning helplessness into the child's eyes, in which there was more blue than formerly.

There came an evening when the soldier took his usual place, carrying with him a handful of beans which he himself had gathered in the moonlit garden. The child accepted them with a wan smile, and after swallowing one or two, said in English the word: 'Grace.'

Then a change came over his face, and reaching out he took the stick which leaned against the knight's leg, and gazed long at the face which was carved on it. And to himself he murmured one word in his own tongue.

'Amabel,' said the soldier, 'what does he say?'

The boy murmured again, and the girl said, her face thin with dread: 'He says: "Green." He says: "Home." He says: "Green home."'

The boy's green-blue eyes, fixed on the carved face, slowly closed. With his free hand he touched the knight's crippled knee, and then he died.

The soldier and the girl, leaving him to the priest and the woman, went out into the garden. And under the stars and the moon, looking up, the knight said: 'There, perhaps, he goes, into that awful vastness, where the warrior-archangel will receive him with loving-kindness and guide him to his green home.'

As a star fell, the girl, who had been disturbingly still, burst into a passion of tears. The soldier, with tears on his own lean cheeks, clutched her to him, and stroking her hair, which in the moonlight was blonde, said: 'Oh Amabel, oh little Mirabel. There are more green homes than one.'

Seven years passed. The girl, growing perfect in our tongue, also most surprisingly showed herself at fourteen very skilled in music, and a scholar the equal of any abbess in the land. The priest somewhat ruefully admitted her his superior. Yet she was no abbess in the making, but chambermaid to the lady and nursemaid to her little daughter, and as a foundling and a stranger there was no girl or man on the manor who did not think her of lower station.

Among the youths of the manor was one Robin, a dark lad of pleasing and humorous countenance, foster-brother to the knight's son Mark. For months he had watched the girl with an admiration in which there was something curious and sly.

And one day in late May he said to her: 'Mirabel, you used to be partial to beans. Shouldn't you like to come with me and smell the beanfield in flower?'

When they came to the beanfield, the sweetness of it was an intoxication to the girl, and she stood among the flowers with her elfin face rapt, as if ecstatic with wine. Her skin, by that time, was between green and white, as at that moment the elderflower was. Her fair hair, though streaked with green, had turned lightest blonde, and her eyes were a confusion of green and hazel.

The boy Robin, with a secretive grin, loosened the drawstring of his linen breeches, and said: 'Hey, Mirabel, ever seen one of these?'

The girl's beautiful eyes showed shock, and some disgust. But the boy, quite gently yet with his customary indifference, simply clasped her and laid her down among the beanflowers.

Long afterwards, Robin told everything to a crony. 'She have all the clothes off me,' he said. 'It was like she want to swallow me whole. She keep calling out in her foreign lingo. And she say: "Oh, you're warm," she say, "you're mine." She say: "Robin, love me, love me." She say: "Oh, I was alone." When I couldn't do no more, she just hold me like a baby, and she say: "You're mine," she say "you're mine." '

For weeks after that the green girl and the dark boy were lovers. But because of her strange intensity, or because, more likely, of a coolness in his own nature, he began to avoid her, and took up with Margery, she who was the laughing-stock of the dairy because, for beauty's sake, she had been seen to wash herself in milk. For a long time thereafter the green girl seemed in her inscrutable way to mourn. But some yearning had been awakened in her by the lad's body, and when cheerfulness returned she became (as the knight afterwards told the Lord Abbot) *nimium lasciva et petulans*, that is, very lascivious and wanton.

125

One day the girl came upon Roger, the man who had been lord of the harvest when she and her brother were discovered, alone in a wood, sitting on a log to take his noonday bread and beer. She seated herself beside him, and accepted some beer. At last the man broke his silence to ask a question which had been in his mind for nearly eight years. 'Tell me straight, gal, where was you and young Mikey from?'

Without answering, the girl took the knife from his waist, and choosing a piece of rotten wood began very skilfully to carve. When she had finished, she showed the man her work.

'Oh-ah,' said Roger. 'A woman, and up the stick.'

The rude figure was indeed of a grinning woman, large-breasted and hugely pregnant.

'That,' the girl said, 'is our goddess. We were children of the flint-mines. Day after day, year after year, century after century, we crawled along the galleries of our mines, loosening flints with our picks made from the antlers of red deer. I do not understand our life. I do not understand how we came here. But suddenly we found ourselves in that pit, in the blinding sun and stunning heat, and could discover no hole leading back to the gallery. And so we lay there weeping, until seized away.'

'I do believe,' said Roger, 'that you might be talking about Grime's Graves.'

'I have never heard that name,' the girl said. 'I remember only our mines and galleries, and our goddess, before whose figure carved in chalk a little lamp burned.'

'And what about your god?' asked Roger, and sniggered. 'She didn't get that way on her own, if I recall the facts of life.'

The girl took up the knife again, and turning aside, her long greenish-fair hair dangling, began to carve once more. When she had finished, she held out to Roger a phallus, the glans and testicles painstakingly distinct.

'That,' she said, 'is our god.'

126

'Something tell me,' said Roger, 'I sin him before. Yes, and not so very far from here.'

For answer the girl pulled the drawstring of his breeches.

Afterwards she said, or pleaded: 'Roger, you love me?'

'Love?' said the taciturn man. 'Why, gal, that int one of my words. But,' he said, giving her a slap on the rump, 'I'll say this for you, you int a bad little old poke.'

The girl liked to haunt the woods and the heaths, and in another wood one day the soldier, walking for exercise of his leg, found her lying among last year's leaves. Over her head an elderbush, its flowers in their last fragile fullness, smelled overpoweringly heavy.

'Mirabel,' he said, with the help of his stick and with a little difficulty sitting beside her, 'Mirabel, you are no longer a green girl. You are the fairest and whitest of girls, as white as elderflower.'

The girl said nothing, but taking the knight's stick she gazed intently at the carved face, as the dying boy had done, a memory which softened the melancholy soldier.

'This,' she said, 'is our god.'

'A strange god,' said the knight. 'One would say a cruel one.'

'He is,' said the girl, 'the bringer into being, and the destroyer. He is neither cruel nor merciful, but dances for joy at the variousness of everything that is.'

'Then, Mirabel,' said the knight, 'having said so much, you may tell me now from where you and Michael came.'

The girl thought, and taking his hand, once so sunburned and strong, now so thin, she said: 'I shall tell you.

'We are people,' she said, 'of the land of the Antipodes, where, years ago, a man from your world made a visit. He was a swineherd of Derbyshire, and had lost a sow of great value, about to farrow down. In dismay at the thought of the steward's anger, he followed it to a certain cave near the Peak,

127

which is called in the British tongue *With Guint*, and in English the Devil's Arse, because of a violent wind which blows from it continually. Overcoming his fear, the swineherd traced the swine into the cave, and as at that time it was free of wind, he followed long and long through the darkness. At last he came upon a lighted place, and from there emerged into a fair land of spacious fields, where he found reapers harvesting the ripe corn, and among the hanging ears of corn recognized his sow, which had brought forth her litter.

'Marvelling and congratulating himself on this event, the swineherd spoke for a time with the chief man of our land, letting him know what had occurred. And then, taking a joyful leave, he returned with his charges into the darkness of the cave.

'Emerging from its mouth, fresh from the harvest fields of the Antipodes, he was amazed to find that in Derbyshire winter frosts persisted everywhere. And some have said that the winter sun is not the real sun, but as it were a deputy. But of this I understand nothing, though of the swineherd's visit I have often heard, but only know that Michael and I, straying into a cave and wandering far through the darkness, found ourselves at length not in Derbyshire but in Suffolk, in great affright and with mourning for our land which will never see us again.'

'Poor child,' said the knight, and stroked her elder-soft hair. 'But mourn no more, my pretty.'

The girl bent her head to kiss his other hand, and then looked at him with eyes in which there was only one meaning.

Long afterwards, kneeling beside his lean body, she kissed his scarred and twisted leg (for for her pleasure he had made himself naked as a worm), and cried: 'Oh my fair love, oh my warm, wounded love.'

And that was not the last time that the knight and the girl had such commerce. But a sort of shame was on him, because of his wife and because the girl, so young, had grown up in his household. So ever afterwards there was in company a constraint between them, and on some evenings in the hall the girl would look at him with leaf-shaped eyes in which there was a little hurt, but more compassion.

In the hall one winter night, seated with the priest before the fire, the girl took up the lady's harp and sang a hymn, beginning:

> *Martine te deprecor,*
> *Pro me rogaris Patrem,*
> *Christum ac Spiritum Sanctum*
> *Habentem Mariam matrem.*

Which is in English:

> Saint Martin, I beseech thee,
> For me entreat the Father,
> Christ Jesu and the Holy Ghost
> Who Mary had for mother.

When she had ended, the priest said: 'A beautiful hymn. Where have you learned it?'

'It came out of Ireland,' said the girl, 'I believe. But it might be a song of my own land, for Saint Martin is the chief saint among us.'

'Indeed?' said the priest. 'Then there are churches in your land?'

'Many, many churches,' said the girl, 'all dedicated to Saint Martin. But our churches do not shine like yours. In our land there is little light, but as it were a perpetual gloaming, and not far from us is a certain luminous country, divided from us by a great stream.'

'Indeed?' repeated the priest. 'Then I take you for one of the Antoikoi or the Antichthones, who live south of the equatorial ocean. And I think that the land you have seen is the edge of Africa, lighted from above like the rim of a plate, by the sun which never descends to your hemisphere.'

'Of that I understand nothing,' said the girl, 'nor of how my brother and I came here. I only know that we were minding our father's flock, and strayed into a cave.' And after wandering far, we heard a certain delectable sound of bells, as when in Bury they all chime together, and at the sound we were entranced, caught up in the spirit, and knew no more until we found ourselves near the harvest field.'

'And the people of your land,' said the priest, 'they are all green, these Christians?'

'Yes,' said the girl, 'green in every part and member. As I was once, and am still, between my thighs.'

The girl looked at the priest with eyes in which there was only one question. The priest's own eyes were shadowed. Though his body was large, his mouth was that of a good little boy.

'Would you love me?' asked the girl.

'No, Mirabel,' said the priest, tearing his wistful eyes away from the hazel mists of hers, and staring at his own clasped hands. 'It would be sin, it would be folly, it would be pain. But,' he said, and gazed at her again with a boyish candour, 'I have loved you, and do, as no other child of God. So try me no more, but believe in my love, and I shall bring you from Bury, done by a clever monk there, the hymn to Saint Martin with a picture of the saint dividing his cloak with the beggar. And the naked man will be green, and will look like Michael.'

The soldier's son, now a clerk of nineteen years, came to visit his parents and his sister. And by strategy he waylaid Mirabel beside a haystack.

'Tell me,' he said, 'of Saint Martin, your land's patron saint.'

The girl looked at the coltish youth with a shrewd under-

130

standing. 'On top of the stack,' she said, 'that is where I will tell you.'

When they lay side by side, she said: 'Saint Martin is of the Devil.'

'Holy Virgin!' exclaimed the clerk. 'This is heresy.'

'We, who are ancient Britons,' said the girl, 'call him Merddin. He was begotten of Satan upon a nun, and is the high priest of his father, whom in our orgies we name Manogan. And in Manogan's name we dye our skins green, for that is his favoured colour, and in that colour he appears at our conventicles, or rites, to take his pleasure of woman or man.

'For long after Christianity came to the British countries, Merddin lay asleep beneath the earth in a forest of Brittany called Brocelien, which in our tongue means "the land of concealment". But in time he rose again, and gave his name as Martin, and was made bishop of Tours. He was the son, he said, of Florus the Hun, and therefore first cousin to the Seven Sleepers, whom Martin ordained, and sent into the cave where they lie breathing still. Their turning in their sleep, as happened in the time of Edward the Confessor and was miraculously made known to him, is a portent of dreadful calamities in the world, but happens perhaps once in two centuries.

'The bishop Saint Martin was a potent sorcerer, as Christians may read. When the Emperor Valentinian refused to receive him, he passed with the aid of a demon through bolts and bars, and stood suddenly before the throne. And when the great monarch would not rise to greet him, flames covered that seat and scorched him *ea parte corporis qua sedebat*, that is, on the part of the body where he sat down.

'Christians also know of my people because of Priscillian, who travelled Gaul with processions of women, before whom he appeared naked to perform his rites, his magical orgies and obscene discourses. In such a fashion we honour Manogan, or Satan, and his son Merddin, or Saint Martin, who is not dead but sleeps in a prison of air beneath a hawthorn.'

The long-legged youth moved yet closer to the girl, and panting said: 'Mirabel, let us honour Saint Martin.'

'Kiss me,' said the girl.

The youth kissed her, long and long, lying upon her body. But suddenly he groaned, and rolled away.

'It is no matter,' said the girl, gazing with her strange eyes into the sky. 'The god knows that all things rise again.'

But the youth was shamed. 'I don't want to,' he muttered, 'now. It is sin, it is the risk of eternal perdition.' And leaping down from the stack, he made his way home to the manor house, and never saw the green girl again.

A pedlar came to the manor, a young man with brown curling hair, and was well received by all the women, for the sake of his gewgaws but also for himself, for his tongue was sharp but his smile was warm, and he seemed to admire all of them. But most often his sea-grey eyes were on the green girl.

He slept that night among the straw in the stables, and when all the household was abed the girl came to him. He drew her down to where he lay naked, and long and joyously they honoured Saint Martin.

When they were still, the girl murmured, stroking his shaggy chest: 'Oh love me, love me. I am alone. Oh, be mine.'

'I am yours,' said Matthew, for that was his name, 'and love you truly, and we shall never part.'

She buried her face in his breast, and sobbed, as when she was new to our world.

'You are strange,' said her lover. 'You are like no one else here. Tell me from where you came.'

The girl meditated, listening to the stirring of the horses. 'I shall tell you,' she said, 'when I know all there is to know of you.'

'Of me?' said the young man, and she glimpsed his white wild-man's grin. 'If you keep secrets, as I am sure you do, I shall tell you. I am a Jew of Lynn.'

At the bleakness in his voice, she comforted him with her whole body.

'How much of the blame,' said Matthew, 'for the fate of our people, for the horrors of York, may lie on a single man. I do not mean King Richard, though his favour was soon a curse to us. I mean one Jew of Lynn, who chose for himself the Christian faith, so enraging the rich and numerous Jewish merchants of the town that in their arrogance they took up arms against him, and calling him deserter and renegade, pursued him to a Christian church. It was for our sake that he fled the house, for he was my father.

'The huge noise, as they besieged the church and broke down the doors, and dragged my father away to punishment, attracted many Christians, who already hated us for our wealth and pride and the King's favours. And many came running with arms, among them a crowd of young strangers from the ships, who traded in Lynn. And all of them fell upon our people, who could not withstand them. Many were hewn down in flight, and with them my father, though whether a Jew or a Christian killed him I shall never know.

'From there the Christians went to our houses, looting and killing, and at last burning everywhere. So my mother and brothers and sisters died, either by fire or the sword. That night, since I was at Norwich, there was not a living Jew in Lynn.

'The next day a Jewish physician arrived, a man much respected by Christians for his art and manners. But in his grief he expressed himself immoderately, seeming to prophesy revenge, and so the Christians made him the last victim of the Jewish fever. And the young foreigners, laden with our wealth, made off again in their ships, and on them the people of Lynn blame everything.'

'And yet,' said the green girl softly, 'you live there still.'

'I should have gone,' said Matthew. 'I should have gone to York. If only that had been my fate. I would have died with

133

them proudly, by my own hand. Masada,' he murmured to himself, in a voice like a groan. 'Masada.'

'And what have you to return to,' the girl asked, 'there in Lynn?'

'A hut by the sea,' said the young man. 'A squalid hut, for me orphaned by riches. I am pedlar or sailor or what work comes to hand. I am not known to be a Jew. We were so many, I was not noticed among so many. Now we are one.'

He stopped, his breath coming fast, then rolled on his side to face her. 'And you, my Mirabel?'

'We were people,' said the girl, in her quietest voice, 'of a far foreign land, which I think you would call Tartary. As children, my brother and I were stolen away. We were brought by sailors to Ipswich to be sold as slaves.'

The young man stroked her hair, all his speech in his eyes.

'There we escaped,' said the girl, 'and lived in the woods, on the heaths. We were very young. How long it lasted is all unclear. We lived like deer or squirrels, on whatever fruit or green things we dared try. The greatest joy I remember was discovering a field of beans.

'As we weakened, our skins began to change. We became green children. When we fell into the pit near the harvest field, we were weak to the point of death. And my brother's end I attribute to that weakness, that long green hunger.'

'Mirabel,' said the young man, 'are you telling me the truth?'

'Does it matter?' asked the girl, with a shy laugh. 'I have so many truths to tell.'

The young man stood up in his nakedness and searched for his clothes. 'We shall go tonight,' he said. 'To these people who have been kind to you you will write, for I know you can write. But tonight you and I must vanish, vanish for ever, into a hut by the sea at Lynn.'

The girl rose beside him, and twined around him her

elder-white body. 'Oh my love,' she said. 'Oh my own one. Oh my home.'

Many years later the priest received from a traveller a grimy letter. 'I am sick and alone,' it said, 'and would wish to speak with you. For the love you vowed, undertake the journey. I am the widow of Matthew Pedlar of Lynn.'

In a hut by the grey winter sea, with a leaking roof and a window rimmed with snow, on a musty bed tossed by fever, the grey-haired priest discovered the green girl. But green no longer, and a girl no longer, for her silken hair was white, and in her wandering eyes there was only a freckling of their old hue.

The priest, kneeling beside her, said the prayer of intercession to Saint Martin, and then the Pater Noster. But she seemed not to understand, nor to know him, so he took her hand and made her his farewell.

'In love is grief,' he said, 'in grief is love. As your grief for him is love, so is my grief for you. Pity my grief. Let my grief teach you to love mankind.

'Truly there is in the world nothing so strange, so fathomless as love. Our home is not here, it is in Heaven; our time is not now, it is eternity; we are here as shipwrecked mariners on an island, moving among strangers, darkly. Why should we love these shadows, which will be gone at the first light? It is because in exile we grieve for one another, it is because we remember the same home, it is because we remember the same father, that there is love in our island.

'In the garden of God are regions of darkness, waste heaths and wan waters, gulfs of mystery, where the bewildered soul may wander aghast. Do not think to rest in your village, in your church, in your land always secure. For God is wider than middle earth, vaster than time, and as His love is infinite, so also is His strangeness. For His love we love Him, and for His strangeness we ought to fear Him, lest to chastise us He bring us into those dark and humbling places.

'I, even I, have known a prodigy and a marvel, and I have wept for two children, and feared in their plight to see an image of my own. Nevertheless I did not despair, for them or for myself, knowing that even in their wandering they rested still in reach of God's hand. For no man is lost, no man goes astray in God's garden; which is here, which is now, which is tomorrow, which is always, time and time again.'

Mirabel's eyes, which had been closed, slowly fluttered open. Into them there seemed to come the paradox of a green flush as she died.

'This I believe and must,' said Jacques Maunoir. 'I believe, and must.'

JUNE

In the bar of the Shoulder of Mutton Clare sat alone. He was barman for the night, but had had no custom since the darts team and its supporters went away, and had settled in the pub's most comfortable chair beside the empty grate.

From his pocket he took two opened letters, and putting aside the long envelope, began to re-read the one with a letterhead from a hotel in Alaska.

Didn't manage to see your friend Jim-Jacques, but he was civil enough to ring my hotel in New York, and we rabbited on a bit. My impression is that you may be addressing letters to Father Maunoir again some day. I don't know – *can* one have two bites at that cherry? He implied he was happy, and sounded it. He thanks you, by the way, for the green kids, whatever that means, and will write.

This town is crazy. At the last – town I couldn't call it, say oasis, for the joke – we stayed in a wooden shack which had *Top Of The World Hotel* painted on a caribou skin tacked to the outside wall. I have Arctic crabs. The quack prescribed a pressure-pack spray, whose instructions begin: 'Hold the nozzle six inches from the beast, and spray particularly around the horns and underparts.'

Tonight I was assaulted in a bar, the first time. It happened like this. There's an Eskimo woman I've got to know slightly, called Dolores (Lolita) Suvik, who became very drunk, because a fellow who had lost a bar-bet bought every man and woman of us there seventeen bottles of beer. So Lolita started making conversation along the lines of: 'I know what you want, all you men are the same, you just want to get up my rectum.' Before you make a fool of yourself in some anthropological journal. I point out that English isn't her first language. Her conversations with her friends seem to consist of the phrase 'Bottled chocolate'll throttle you,' endlessly repeated. Well, she started doing an Eskimo war-dance, which was a solitary business and got in no one's way. But then she fancied something on the jukebox, and wanted to dance with me. Seeing how drunk she was, I clung for dear life to the bar rail, and giving up at last she sat down on the next stool and started growling: 'Goddam white man.' Then she said: 'Goddam white man, are you queer or something?' To this I made what I think quite the best repartee of my life to date, namely: 'Only for you, baby.' She punched me and made my nose bleed.

More in our next. Many happenings to report. Your news always good lately.

Your loving schoolfellow,

M. J. PERRY

Clare slumped more comfortably in the old wooden arm-chair, and looked absently at an advertisement for some feminine drink or cigarette. In a long vista of sun-shot wood-land the backs of two evidently beautiful young people could be seen receding.

He was in the ride leading through Lady Munby's woods. The Alsatian from the farm had brought him there, but the dog had disappeared. He stood irresolute, smelling the drunkenness of a flowering beanfield from nearby.

He was further on in the wood, where the masses of bluebells had lost their earlier darkness and faded to the colour of old denim. Gathering them he saw a small fairhaired girl, and said: 'Amabel.' But the child only smiled, with green-brown leaf-shaped eyes, and was suddenly no longer there.

At another point in the ride he saw a fairhaired woman. She turned, and he realized that it was Alicia in a headscarf. She smiled at him, vaguely, and passed, going to meet someone else.

He was standing in the heavy scent of an elder bush when he saw the back of a girl with long straight hair of elder-cream. As she, like Alicia, turned, he cried out: 'Mirabel!'

Her eyes had not changed, but were still the green of leeks.

'*E*,' she said. '*Kulisapini, ambaesa bu ku?*'

'*Ki*!' he exclaimed. '*Ku nukwali biga!*' He was amazed that she understood the language.

In the same tongue she replied: 'Yes, I speak it. I also am of Saint Martin's Land.'

He was about to approach her, when the door banged, and he woke.

'So this,' said Alicia, 'is how you work for Mr Partridge. I hope he doesn't pay very well.'

'He pays in kind,' Clare said, 'and I'm not thirsty.' His eyes and mind, refocusing after sleep, made of the sylvan advertisement something which he had noted to tell her. 'Lissa, I saw a marvellous thing today at the farmhouse. Eight of their white doves were going crazy over the big elder. Ice-white against yellowish-white. "They're grazing on the bloom," Roger said.'

'I'll think about it,' said Alicia. 'Constable had a fondness for elder, like you. He wrote somewhere: "It is a favourite of mine and always was – but 'tis melancholy."'

'A drink?' he said, going behind the bar, and without waiting for an answer poured two gins. 'By the way, Lissa, I've got a job.'

'Oh, Crispin,' she said, 'I'm so glad. What is it?'

'Academic,' he said, slicing a lemon. 'Failed men of action teach. I can come and see you on that little train that passes the house Malkin haunted. At least, it's a barn now, but I'm sure it was the manor house.'

'You've lost me,' Alicia said. 'What is Malkin?'

'A twelfth-century sprite,' Clare said. 'She once came through on your ouija board. By the way, I think I understand that now. There used to be a horse called Clever Hans which could answer simple questions in arithmetic, by stamping. Not even the owner knew how it was done, but it seems that Hans somehow got messages from the body-tensions of the owner, so he sensed when he was getting warm, and when he was spot-on. I think Amabel works like that. She knew, without knowing, what I expected to see, and wrote it.'

'Unnerving child, as you said,' remarked Alicia. 'But normal.'

Tonic poured fizzing and clinking around the ice. 'A friend of mine thinks Jim-Jacques might go back to being a priest.'

Alicia, reflecting, said: 'That pleases me, somehow. It's my tidy mind, I suppose, essentially Protestant, which wants things in their right place. Jim-Jacques never seemed to me to be anything else but a priest. Beautiful as he is, to one of my years.'

She raised her glass, and Clare chinked his own against it. She looked at him surprised, and he noticed in her eyes, the colour of fine dry sherry, a few flecks of green.

'What is the toast?' she asked.

'I don't know,' he said. 'A general toast. To the place. To seely Suffolk.'

AUTHOR'S NOTE

The stories of the sprite of Dagworth, the wild man of Orford and the green children of Woolpit are reported as recent history in the *Chronicon Anglicanum* of Ralph of Coggeshall (ed. Joseph Stevenson, London, 1875). The story of the green children is also told, with slight additions, by William of Newburgh in his *Historia Rerum Anglicarum* (ed. Hans Claude Hamilton, London, 1856). From William too I have taken the account of the Jews of King's Lynn.

The stories of the Antipodes and their land, and of the Catalan father's curse, are from Gervase of Tilbury's *Otia Imperialia* (ed. Felix Liebrecht, Hanover, 1856). Various other hares were started by Liebrecht's copious notes and quotations.

The story of the merman Nicholas Pipe is from Walter Map's *De Nugis Curialium* (ed. Thomas Wright, London, 1850). 'Annis and the Merman' is a free translation of the Danish ballad 'Agnete og Havmanden', included in Ernst Frandsen's collection *Danske Folkeviser* (Copenhagen, 1966). The Irish-Latin hymn in honour of Saint Martin, by Oengus, is taken from William Beare's *Latin Verse and European Song* (London, 1957), and the aspersions on Saint Martin's character can be read in *Britannia After The Romans*, published anonymously in two volumes (London, 1836 and 1841) by the Hon. Algernon Herbert. The source of the charm against Old Shuck

I have been unable to rediscover, but am most grateful to Victoria Hyde for sending it to me.

R.S.

APPENDIX

Concerning a fantastic sprite

In the time of King Richard, at Dagworth in Suffolk, in the house of Master Osbern Bradwell, a fantastic sprite repeatedly and for a considerable time appeared, speaking with the family of the aforesaid soldier, mimicking in sound the voice of a child one year old, and she called herself Malkin. She asserted that her mother lived with her brother in a neighbouring house, and said that she was frequently scolded by them because, forsaking them, she chose to speak with mankind. She both spoke and acted in a way wonderfully laughable, often uncovering the hidden deeds of others. At first the soldier's wife and the whole household were much frightened by her speeches, but being afterwards accustomed to her ridiculous words and acts, they spoke confidently and familiarly with her, inquiring of her many things. She spoke English in the dialect of that region, and now and then Latin, and she held forth upon the Scriptures with the soldier's chaplain, as he has often truthfully affirmed to us. She could be heard and felt, but not in the least way seen, except that once, by a certain chambermaid, she was seen in the aspect of a very small child, dressed in a white tunic, the girl having previously much beseeched and adjured her to make herself visible. To which petition she would in no wise consent, until the girl swore by the Lord that she would neither touch her nor hold her. She avowed that she was born at Lavenham, and that

145

when her mother took her into a field, where she was harvesting with the others, and left her alone in a part of the field, she was seized by a certain other woman and taken away, and had now remained with her for seven years. And she said that after another seven years she would return to her former cohabitation with mankind. She said that she and the others made use of a cap which rendered them invisible. She frequently demanded food and drink of the servitors, which, when it had been placed upon a certain chest, was discovered no more.

Ralph of Coggeshall (fl. A.D. 1187–1218):
Chronicon Anglicanum

Concerning a wild man caught in the sea

In the times of King Henry the Second, when Bartholomew Glanville was constable of Orford Castle, it happened that some fishermen of that place fishing in the sea captured among their nets a wild man; who being brought before the aforesaid constable out of wonder, was naked in every part and pretended to the human form in all members. He had, moreover, hairs, but they seemed on the upper face as if plucked and cast away; his beard was trúly abundant and like feathers; and about his chest he was very hairy and shaggy. For a very long time the aforesaid constable had him guarded by day and by night, lest he should approach the sea. What was put before him he ate avidly. Fish, indeed, he ate raw as well as cooked, but the raw ones he squeezed strongly between his hands until the moisture was all consumed, and then he ate them. He would utter no speech, or rather could not, even though hung by the feet and often most horribly tortured. Although brought to the church, he showed not the least sign of veneration or of any faith, either by genuflexion or by bowing of the head, however often he perceived the sacred things. At sundown he always hastily sought his bed, lying there until sunrise. It happened that they once led him to the haven, and loosed him into the sea, having first placed before him very strong nets in a triple line. Soon seeking the depths of the sea, and penetrating all the nets, he emerged again and again from the bottom of the sea, and for a long time watched the watchers on the shore, often submerging, and a little afterwards emerging, as if scoffing at the onlookers because he had escaped their nets. And when he had long disported himself in the sea in this way, and all hope of his return had been cast aside, of his own free will he returned to them on the sea's billows, swimming, and once more remained with them for two months. But as he was afterwards more negligently guarded, and was now held in aversion, he fled away secretly to the sea, and was nowhere seen again. As to whether this was a mortal man, or some fish pretending human shape, or was a malign spirit hiding in the body of a drowned man, as can be read of in the life of blessed Ouen, it is not possible to be precise; the more so because so many wonderful things of this kind are told by so many to whom they have happened.

Ralph of Coggeshall

Concerning a boy and girl emerging from the earth

Another also wondrous thing, not unlike the foregoing, happened in Suffolk at St Mary Woolpit. A certain boy was discovered with his sister by the inhabitants of that place, lying by the edge of a pit which exists there, who had the same form in all members as the rest of mankind, but in the colour of their skins differed from all mortals of our habitable world. For the whole surface of their skins was tinged with a green colour. Nobody could understand their speech. Being accordingly brought out of wonder to the house of Master Richard Calne, a soldier, at Wikes, they wept inconsolably. Bread and other food was brought to them, but they would eat no victuals which were placed before them, even while tormented for a long time by the greatest pangs of hunger, because all food of that kind they believed to be inedible, as the girl afterwards

147

avowed. At length, when some beans newly broken off with their stalks were brought into the house, they made signs with the greatest avidity that those beans should be given to them. Which being brought to them, they opened the stalks in place of the bean-pods, thinking the beans to be contained in the hollow of the stalks. This some of those standing by noticed, and opened the pods and showed the naked beans, which being shown they ate with great joy, for a long time touching no other food at all. The boy, however, always as it were oppressed by languor, after a short time died. But the girl, enjoying continual good health, and become used to any kind of food, entirely lost that leek-green colour, and gradually recovered a sanguine habit of the whole body. She afterwards being regenerated by the holy bath of baptism, and remaining for many years in the service of the aforesaid soldier (as from the soldier and his household we frequently heard), showed herself very lascivious and wanton. Questioned frequently concerning the men of her region, she averred that all dwellers and things in that region were tinged with a green colour, and that they perceived no sun, but enjoyed a certain brightness such as happens after sunset. Questioned further by what means she had come into this land with the aforesaid boy, she replied that because they were following some cattle, they came into a cave. Having entered which, they heard a certain delectable sound of bells; caught up by the sweetness of which sound, they walked for a long time wandering through the cavern, until they came to the exit of it. Whence emerging, as if stunned by the too great brightness of the sun and unaccustomed temperature of the air, they lay long at the edge of the grotto. And when they were terrified by the agitation of those who came upon them, they wished to flee, but could in no wise discover the entrance of the cave, before they were seized by those arrivals.

Ralph of Coggeshall

Nor does it seem proper to pass over a prodigy unheard of by generations which is known to have happened in England under King Stephen. And indeed I have hesitated long over this matter, which was related by many; and the thing seemed to me either of no or of concealed reason, ridiculous to repose faith in; until so overwhelmed by the weight of so many and such witnesses as to be compelled to believe and marvel at what I cannot approach or explain by any forces of the intellect. There is a village in East Anglia four or five miles distant, it is said, from the noble monastery of the blessed king and martyr Edmund. Near which village are seen certain very ancient pits, which are called in the English tongue *Wlfpittes*, that is, the pits of the wolves, and bestow their name upon the village which they adjoin. Out of those pits at the time of the harvest, the reapers being busy about the gathering of the fruits throughout the fields, there emerged two children, male and female, green in the whole body and of strange hue, clad in raiment of unknown material. And when they were wandering stunned through the field, they were seized by the reapers and led into the village, and with many tears at the sight of so much which was novel, for several days were tried with offered food. When they were almost dead with fasting, nor attended to any of the foods which were offered to them, by chance some beans happened to be brought from the field; which immediately seizing, they sought the lentil itself in the stalks, and finding nothing in the hollow of the stalks, wept bitterly. Then certain of those who were present offered them the legume plucked out of the shells; which immediately accepting, they ate freely. They were nourished by this food for several months, until they knew the use of bread. Thereupon, little by little changing their own colour, through the prevailing nature of our foods, and rendered like us, they also learned the use of our language. And it seemed to the wise that they should receive the sacrament of holy baptism, which indeed was done. But the boy, who seemed to be the younger, living a short time after the baptism, was removed by premature death; his sister, however, remaining safe and sound, nor differing in much from the women of our kind. Indeed, she afterwards took a husband at Lynn, it is said, and a few years ago was said to be still living. When they had the use of our tongue, being asked who and whence they were, they are stated to have replied: 'We are people of the land of Saint Martin, who undoubtedly is held in especial veneration in the land of our birth.' Subsequently asked where that land might be, and by what means they had come from thence, they said: 'We know neither. This much we remember: that when one day we were grazing our father's cattle in a field, we heard a certain great sound, as we are now accustomed to hear at St Edmunds, when they are said to sound the tocsin. And when we heard that sound which we wondered at in our souls, suddenly, as if fallen into some departure of the mind, we found ourselves among you in the field where you were reaping.' Asked whether in that place there was belief in Christ, or whether the sun rose, they said that land to be Christian and to have churches. 'But the sun,' they said, 'does not rise in our native places; its rays illumine our land very slightly, restricted to a measure of that brightness which among you either precedes the sun in the east or follows it in the west. Moreover, a certain lighted land is seen not far from our land, the two being divided by a very broad stream.' These and many other things, long to unravel, they are reported curiously to have replied to those inquiring, and let what conclusions that can be drawn concerning these matters. I myself am not ashamed to have set forth the prodigious and marvellous event.

William of Newburgh (A.D. 1136–ca. 1198):
Historia Rerum Anglicarum